THE GOLDEN DOOR

Charles B. Nam

THE GOLDEN DOOR

Charles B. Nam

iUniverse, Inc.

New York Lincoln Shanghai

The Golden Door

Copyright © 2006 by Charles B. Nam

iUniverse books may be ordered through booksellers or by contacting:

iUniverse
2021 Pine Lake Road, Suite 100
Lincoln, NE 68512
www.iuniverse.com
1-800-Authors (1-800-288-4677)

ISBN-13: 978-0-595-39650-4 (pbk)
ISBN-13: 978-0-595-84054-0 (ebk)
ISBN-10: 0-595-39650-X (pbk)
ISBN-10: 0-595-84054-X (ebk)

Printed in the United States of America

"Keep ancient lands, your storied pomp!" cries she
With silent lips, "Give me your tired, your poor,
Your huddled masses yearning to breathe free,
The wretched refuse of your teeming shore.
Send these, the homeless, tempest-tost to me,
I lift my lamp beside the golden door!"

—Emma Lazarus, from *The New Colossus*

Acknowledgments

Several people helped shape this book into its present form. My late wife, Marjorie Tallant Nam, read my original prospectus for the story and provided criticisms as well as encouragement. Judy Gross edited the complete first draft of the manuscript and introduced a novice fiction writer to fundamentals of the craft. Maxine Stern, Richard Dempsey, and Delia Wright read different versions of the manuscript and provided useful comments. Margaret Barlow edited a later draft and served to make the text more readable. Stan Corwin's suggestions to expand and refine the text were welcomed. I am entirely responsible for whatever shortcomings remain.

Introduction

In the peak years of late Nineteenth and early Twentieth Century immigration to the United States, passengers arrived at a number of different ports, but the vast majority came to New York. The ships they were on entered New York Harbor and passed the Statue of Liberty. This statue, about which Emma Lazarus wrote in her poem "The New Colossus," sits on Liberty Island (originally Bedloe's Island). The "grand lady" faces the incoming ships. She holds a facsimile of the Declaration of Independence in her left hand and raises a torch high in her right hand. They are symbols of the values many immigrants to the United States sought for a couple of centuries. The light in Liberty's torch beckons new arrivals to the "Golden Door" on the threshold of the land of freedom and opportunity.

The statue was a gift from France to America in the late Nineteenth Century. It strengthened the bond between two nations that had undergone revolutions against royalty and oppression in the Eighteenth Century. The original name of the statue was *Liberty Enlightening the World*. It was one of the first things immigrants to New York saw on coming to this country. A smaller model of the statue is located on the Seine River in Paris.

Immigration to the United States began long before the Statue of Liberty was created. America was known as a "nation of immigrants." Between 1820 (when statistics on immigrants were first collected) and 1955, more than 40 million aliens entered the United States and more than four fifths of these were from the European continent. The largest waves of these movements entered in the period between 1880 and 1914.

Included in the immigration of that period were substantial numbers of Jews. They constituted more than two million of the arrivals, largely from Eastern Europe and mostly from the Russian Empire.

Throughout history, Jews were on the receiving end of harsh treatment. The condition in the Russian Empire was especially severe. The Russian Czars and their governments disliked all strangers, but particularly hated the Jews, whom they regarded as foreigners, even though Jewish families had lived in the area for longer than 800 years.

The Czars specified a part of the Empire where Jews could live, referred to as the "Pale of Settlement." The Pale covered parts of what are now Poland, Lithuania, Ukraine, Belarus, Latvia, and Russia, but excluded the major cities (such as Moscow and St. Petersburg). Jews represented only ten percent of the population of the Pale, but they were segregated into small villages (called "shtetls") or specified quarters of cities.

These shtetls and Jewish quarters were very crowded and travel outside the area was not permitted. Only certain occupations could be practiced by Jews. Residents were taxed heavily and armed attacks by Cossacks or massacres by neighboring Gentiles (usually prompted by the Czarist government) were frequent. Jewish resistance groups proved powerless and the only alternatives were religious conversion or emigration.

The few immigrants who had the economic means would occupy rooms in first or second class compartments and enjoyed some comforts on the journey that took from ten days to a month or more. Most of the immigrants would be found in a section of the ship called "steerage." These passengers were crammed together in small spaces. They had meager rations and inadequate toilet and bathing facilities. Seasickness was common, but the victims had little or no recourse to medications.

New York City was the favorite destination for Eastern European Jews. Fully two thirds of all Jewish immigrants ended up in New York and stayed there. A small number of Jewish arrivals were economically secure and managed to acquire or establish businesses. But for every financially independent Jew, there were thousands more whose poverty meant they lived from month to month without a promise of better times ahead. For each Jewish business leader or professional, there were thousands more who eked out a living as tailors, sewing machine operators, peddlers, dock workers, or at other low paying jobs.

The story which follows is fictional, but it is based on a few facts about a real immigrant journey that took place in the early 1890s. Names of the real ship, the real persons, and the real places have been changed. But the story tells what might very well have happened.

CHAPTER 1

▼

"Do you remember?" Mrs. Newman said to her daughter Sarah.

"Remember what I told your father? Watch out for that man. He's no good. The way he looked at you and Feyga. *Ayin horeh.* The whole time we were on that boat."

"But Momma, nothing happened. We all made it safe to America. You're a worrier. Nothing happened."

"OK, OK. We'll wait and see. The evil eye. Once it looks at you, it never stops. You children mean everything to me. Your Poppa and me, we've got to make sure you have a good, long life."

"Sure, Momma. Stop worrying, Momma. We're here. Let's be happy.

(*Two years later*)

The two young women made their way toward Battery Park. Sarah and Molly carried metal framed cloth pocketbooks bulging with personal items and food they hadn't had time to eat before leaving home.

They headed toward the ferryboat. Workers heading for the factories in Staten Island and New Jersey rushed past them to catch the ferry. Sarah and Molly sauntered slowly. They were not in a hurry. They were on a special mission.

After a short distance, Sarah nudged Molly and grabbed her hand. "No, *this* is the way to the dock. I remember it from before." They headed off in a slightly different direction.

"Ya know, I could hardly sleep last night. Every time I dozed off, I sat up in bed and looked at the clock to make sure I hadn't missed hearing the alarm."

"I know what you mean," said Molly. "I was kind of fidgety myself last night."

Sarah looked around. The rising sun reflected on the bay and pierced the haze covering the southern tip of Manhattan Island. The early morning quiet gave way to sounds of the dock. One could hear the sloshing of barges carrying crates of produce from distant ports, the musical calls of ferries filled with nightshift workers going home, the squealing of winches and sails, and the stretching and moaning of wooden piles at the pier.

"It's an exciting place, isn't it?" remarked Sarah. "Just think, two years ago me and my family came to New York. I remember how awful it was on the ship."

Molly chimed in, "We came *four* years ago to Castle Garden, but it seems like yesterday. We used to be the "greenhorns" and now we're the old timers waiting for a new batch of "greenhorns.""

"We must've looked funny when we got off the boat. It was the Barge Office then. If we didn't take that English course, we'd still be greenhorns. At least now, we don't sound like we just got here."

At the street leading to the pier, the morning activity was more lively. Horse carts rolled by weighed down by heavy cargoes of crates and gunny sacks. Workers were rushing to offices and factories. The steam powered elevated railway stopped hissingly to take on new passengers. A newspaper boy still half asleep waved his wares and called out, "Get your morning paper here!"

When Sarah and her family arrived in New York in 1891, they were impressed with its hugeness and extraordinary sights—the vast New York Harbor full of ships of all sizes and types, the imposing Statue of Liberty in its midst, the unusual skyline of the city with its tall buildings.

Manhattan Island was then New York City. Plans were afoot to annex the City of Brooklyn and the boroughs of the Bronx, Queens, and Staten Island.

Sarah could see that the city held a large number of people, a fact her parents knew well before they came, but she was not aware of how rapidly the number of people was growing. Immigrants like themselves had swollen the number of New Yorkers. Already the largest city in the country, in fact in the Western Hemisphere, New York had one and a half million people by that time. Brooklyn had half as many and was becoming especially attractive as an escape from the more densely occupied Manhattan.

What was even more apparent was the growing ethnic diversity of the population. Molly had once remarked how her family had never seen so many people from different countries on the ship they came on. Each of these groups was adding to the number of their countrymen who had come earlier.

To strengthen their cultural bonds and provide mutual aid, those from a particular country tended to settle in the same neighborhoods of the city and maintain many of the customs they brought with them from the old country.

The English and Christian Germans, who mostly came to the city in earlier times, were scattered about the area but dominated the higher rent districts of the city and outlying areas.

The Irish, who came in a later wave and were less affluent, occupied sections of the city below Canal Street. As they rose in the status ladder, they moved uptown or to Brooklyn. Staying together in a neighborhood was important because they could share Irish traditions and be close to their own Catholic churches.

Italians, who along with Eastern European Jews, dominated the newest wave of immigrants, had even more concentrated residential locations, essentially in several political wards north of Canal Street. They further separated themselves by the parts of Italy they came from. Neapolitans and Calabrians were mostly in the Mulberry Bend district, Genoese on Baxter Street, Sicilians on Elizabeth Street between Houston and Spring Streets, North Italians (who generally arrived in the city earlier) were on Sullivan and Thompson Streets. South Italians occupied the stretch of 110th to 115th Streets, known as "Little Italy."

East European Jews lived in the most densely settled section of the city, in three wards on the Lower East Side. In contrast with German Jews, who had come in an earlier immigrant wave, were more prosperous, and occupied less densely settled parts of the city, Jews from the Russian Empire were packed in the tenements of those wards. Among them, as well, were separate sections for those from a particular "shtetl," or village, whose religious practices and traditions of daily living mirrored what had existed in their European quarters.

As the women neared the pier landing, Sarah became quiet. She turned around to take in the view on all sides.

"It's strange being back here, waiting for Julius. I keep thinking back to the time momma and poppa and me arrived in New York. Poor momma. She suffered so much. She hated being on a boat. She acted like it was going to be the end of her days. How many 'Oy's' we heard from her the whole trip! We kept saying, "Momma, momma, it'll be all right. Just think how wonderful it'll be when we get to America.""

Molly laughed. "Yeh, yeh, I can remember the same thing with my family. Daddy was like iron. He seemed to be afraid of nothing. He was probably as scared as the rest of us, but he didn't show it. We looked up to him."

Sarah shook her head and retied her kerchief. "My father was, too. Momma was somethin' else, though. After the trip, we all laughed about it." They chuckled.

Sarah Newman was twenty five, short but with a good figure and a dark complexion that complemented her eyes and hair. She had a good sense of humor with friends and family, but projected a sternness in dealing with others. Those characteristics recommended her for the office job at Manhattan Needleworks Company.

The Jews from Eastern Europe developed various skills that served them well in their ghettoes. Among them was an affinity for needle trades. Both men and women were often engaged in tailoring. They provided clothes for their own families and also sold their services to others. It was not uncommon for family members to work on sewing machines in their own homes, producing finished goods that supplied clothes manufacturers or which they could sell themselves in the market square.

This skill bode well for many of the immigrants to New York. The garment industry, already well established, was booming by 1890 and provided employment for large numbers of the newly arrived. Some cut patterns, others stitched on machines, still others were pressers.

Many of the employers, some of them Jews, took advantage of the immigrants, paying them very low wages, demanding long working hours, and submitting them to difficult, sometimes intolerable, working conditions. Those workers who showed more initiative and had furthered their education were most likely to move out of the production line and acquire more satisfying positions.

After more than a year stitching dresses, Sarah was offered a clerical job. She handled the job well, and her boss, Max Greenstein, was not as demanding as other bosses she'd heard about.

In fact, he was very sympathetic when he learned that Sarah's brother, Julius, was coming from Poland.

"Go ahead and take the day off. It isn't everyday a brother comes. You'll catch up on your work tomorrow."

Of course, there was no pay for a day off, but Sarah was glad to sacrifice. She had missed Julius terribly for two years.

Mr. Greenstein had also allowed Molly Rubin the day off. Molly was Sarah's best friend and co worker. Sarah needed someone to go with her, and other family members were not able to go.

"We'll see him at home soon enough," her father said. "How many in the family can afford to miss a day's work? Maybe the boss will let me slip home at lunchtime."

Molly was the same age as her friend, slightly taller, but with a round face and a perpetual glint in her eye. At the factory, they called her "Sparkle" because she lit up the room when she came in. Always smiling, greeting everyone, she was happy and pleasant in a working environment full of outspoken malcontents and people who suffered in silence.

The two young women went almost everywhere together. They went out with young men from time to time, but neither had met a fellow she could be serious about. They often went to the nightly lectures at Cooper Union. This private college offered free education and it was a great attraction for Jewish immigrants wanting to learn the English language and understand American culture.

On Saturdays, Sarah and Molly often went 'ooh ing' and 'aah ing' through department stores. Intent on making up for their limited formal schooling, they visited the American Museum of Natural History and the Metropolitan Museum of Art. They attended movies whenever they could. The women enjoyed reading romance novels and telling each other about interesting passages. Over tea and home baked cookies, they shared gossip about friends, neighbors, and co workers. The women had even talked about a trip to Chicago to see the newly opened World's Columbian Exposition, celebrating the 400th anniversary of Columbus' discovery of America. It turned out to be too costly, so they sent off for the booklet about it instead.

Opportunities for enjoying life in New York were expanding rapidly. In addition to their standard activities, there were walks in the several small parks on the Lower East Side and attending performances of the new Yiddish Theatre. Acting and singing groups that had performed in Europe recreated their plays and musicals for the immigrant population. On occasion, European musicians traveled to the United States to entertain the public.

Molly turned to Sarah and adjusted the white bow below her chin.

"Here, let me make it straight."

They were both dressed for a special occasion. Sarah had on a dark red cotton dress that reached well below her knees and was cinched at the waist with a thin black belt that matched her half inch heeled button shoes. A large stick pin secured a narrow brimmed black hat to her upswept hair. The skirt on Molly's beige suit fell a bit lower than Sarah's. Her broad brimmed brown hat fit nicely and matched her shoes.

When they reached the park, they found the ferry office on the far side. Cutting through the maze of benches and bushes, they entered the side door. A clerk, tall and lean, wearing a green visor and sporting a pair of dirt guards on his shirtsleeve, shuffled papers behind his desk and paid no attention to them. From time to time, he called out in an Irish brogue to someone in the back room, asking which ferries were on time and which ones were late.

"Excuse me," interrupted Sarah, "d'ya know if the Netherlands has arrived? Has the ferry brought the passengers?"

The clerk turned and, tilting his head, peered over horn rimmed glasses to see who was asking the question.

"I can tell you right now, 'tis nothing I know about the big ships. Sure, it's the ferry business we take care of here. T'were you to ask me about a ferry, I might have an answer now." With a smirk, he returned to sorting through his papers, but he kept glancing at the women, who seemed disappointed.

"Well now, 'tis a relative you're expecting to come in on one of those ships? Sure, they come in every few days and our ferries transport them here to the city, but they don't tell us which ships are arriving."

Molly, her voice rising, asked, "Who can tell us about the ships? We heard that the Netherlands would be here by today, and we are here to meet someone."

The clerk called out to his unseen partner. "Hey, Eddie, what can we tell these young ladies about a big ship? They're here to meet someone and they want to find out if it's come in yet. Isn't that what your buddy, Johnny, deals with at the registry office?"

A burly, ruddy faced man appeared at the door. He peered at the pair, and with a broad smile tipped his hat.

"If you go out this door and walk straight down the pier side, you'll come to the communication office for the ship lines. There's a big sign near the entrance. But there's always a long wait, so why don't you make yourselves comfortable and take a seat in here?" The men leered at their visitors.

"No, thank you," the women said almost in unison. They left promptly through the pier side door. Once outside, Molly said, "What a character! I couldn't get out of there fast enough."

In the early morning light, they could see the building the supervisor described. Halfway there, they looked out at the horizon but could see no large ship. Sarah, heaving a big sigh, sat down on one of the many benches in the park. The weather was pleasant, and it seemed they had time to spare.

"I'm getting hungry," commented Sarah, and she took a pastry wrapped in a napkin out of her bag and placed the bag on her lap to catch the crumbs. She slowly unwrapped the paper and started to nibble.

Reaching into her purse, she withdrew a folded envelope with a foreign stamp. It was the last letter Julius sent, before leaving home to reach the S. S. Netherlands for the voyage to America.

Dear Family,

Soon I will be in France, in Boulogne, waiting for the ship to arrive from Rotterdam. The S. S. Netherlands is scheduled to arrive in New York on May 15. Second class passage was too dear, but steerage is good enough.

Love, Julius

It was a little white lie. Julius knew that was how his parents and sisters sailed for the U.S. and he did not want to give the impression he thought he deserved any better. Moreover, the trip from Boulogne to New York was estimated to take only fourteen days, and he could certainly put up with the inconveniences for that long.

His letter went on:

I am feeling much better these days. Maybe I should have gone with you after all. But that is behind me. Now, I am looking forward to joining you and making our family whole again.

Sarah often mentioned her brother to Molly, but she never told a great deal about him. His earlier letters were full of despair and resignation. Family matters were private. Her parents worried about him. The new letter was much different in tone and Mr. and Mrs. Newman were joyfully planning for Julius' arrival.

"You'll like him a lot," Sarah said, as she reached back into her pocketbook to fetch a photograph of Julius taken a few years earlier. It was one Sarah had showed her friend before. The women stared at the photo before Sarah said pensively, "He's not very tall, but he is handsome, and what deep, dark eyes he has."

"Do you think he'd be interested in me?"

"Why not? You're not a bad looker yourself, and just think what beautiful babies the two of you can make." The two of them laughed uproariously while Molly blushed bright red.

"Ya know Julius has had a hard two years," Sarah went on. "He liked Warsaw better than where we lived in Vilna. He said he liked his work as a pharmacist, but his life was empty. Once we left, he slipped out of the Jewish quarter."

"I know what you're saying. In Kovno, people without families felt strange. Marriage and children was expected. If you had no family, you felt alone. I had a cousin who stayed behind, and that's how he said he felt."

"My parents didn't expect him to remain a serious Jew," Sarah said ruefully, "but they were startled by his conversion. Just think, to have their son become a Catholic. Of course, he had Catholic friends since he was a child and went everywhere with them, but that wasn't unusual in Warsaw.

"Julius is practical. He could see the benefits of converting. You know how hard the Russians were on Jews. That's why we left. But Julius thought the Czarists wouldn't bother him if he converted. He was wrong, though. He thought if he wasn't a Jew, it would be good for business. Again he was wrong. So after almost two years of this going on, he realized once a Jew always a Jew, in your own eyes and the eyes of others.

"We don't ask about his religion now. We're just happy he's coming to join us here."

Molly, breaking off pieces of the bread she had brought along, looked at the photo once more and smiled at Sarah. "The Good Lord works in mysterious ways, they say, so we should wait and see what He has in mind for all of us."

Wrapping the small leftovers in the paper and tossing it in back of the bench, the two of them turned toward the Harbor to see a moderately large ship moving toward Ellis Island. The immigration station had opened just last year. The ship's foghorn sounded across the water.

"Hey, that must be Julius's ship!" Molly beamed. "Let's go to the office and find out when they get off."

CHAPTER 2

▼

Sarah and Molly looked back toward Ellis Island and, for a brief spell, seemed rooted to their places and lost in thought. They grinned at each other, grabbed their belongings, and headed for the office of the ship lines.

As they approached the Registry Office, a small old brick building overgrown with moss and giving off a mildewy smell, they saw some activity just outside. Several men were examining pieces of paper. The women overheard exchanges about the logistics of getting passengers to the mainland. Sarah boldly approached the one who seemed to be in charge.

"Is that the S. S. Netherlands out there?" she asked, pointing toward Ellis Island. "When will the passengers get here?"

"Yeah, that's the Netherlands. Are you waiting for someone from first or second class, or steerage"

When Sarah answered "Steerage," he sneered, "If it's steerage, you'll have a long wait. It'll be hours before they get through processing. If they make it through okay, the ferries will bring them here." He returned to his business.

Sarah remembered what her family had gone through when they came over. Glancing at Molly, she said, "Of course. How can I forget those long lines? After that miserable boat trip, we had to wait and wait and wait. We had to answer all those questions and have our bodies examined. I'll never forget.

"And those poor souls who got rejected. Maybe they didn't meet some tests. Some were even put back on the ship and sent home.

"Of course, there's no reason to worry about Julius. He'll be ready for any question, and he's healthy as a horse," she said brightly.

They returned to the bench, still within eyesight of where the ferries docked. "No use to go home," Molly said. "Let's find a bench with the others."

At mid morning people were arriving to meet relatives and friends. The noise level rose. The crowd assembled in the park near where Sarah and Molly waited, some seated on benches, others standing. Sarah could tell from their clothing and faces that many of them had come from Eastern Europe, but others were clearly from elsewhere.

Pungent aromas of garlic, fried fish, pickles, and bananas filled the air and made nostrils quiver. The sound of so many languages clashing was different from their street, where most of the neighbors spoke Yiddish or Polish.

Molly thought she recognized Mrs. Cohen, a neighbor, but she was engaged in a spirited conversation and didn't notice the two young women.

Not far from Sarah and Molly was a family, speaking loudly in Yiddish. One woman was talking about someone named Abe Solomon. After a few minutes, Sarah asked in English if they were waiting for someone on the S. S. Netherlands.

"Yes, actually two someones," said Irving Goetz. A bright teenager who attended the public school on Houston Street, he was dressed in a white shirt and blue tie and knickers. A small cap sat jauntily on the side of his head, covering straight black hair.

"Our cousins. We're here to greet them."

At that point, one of the older women moved closer. In a heavily accented Eastern European voice, she said, "Hello, I'm Sheyna Goetz, and these are my children, Irving, Joshua, and Charlie. Our cousins, Abraham Solomon and Rivka Borchowitz, are arriving together."

"Mrs. Goetz, I'm Sarah Newman, and this is my friend, Molly Rubin." Heads nodded all around.

"We arrived ourselves just a few years ago," continued Sheyna, "and this is our third time meeting relatives from the old country. Abe and Rivka have jobs waiting for them. Abe's a tailor and Rivka sews beautifully.

"We'll be glad to see them here. The sooner they can get out of that dreadful place, the better. And who are you waiting for?"

Sarah answered, leaving out the details of her brother's situation.

At Joshua's squeal, all heads turned to the sight of a ferryboat easing its way to the pier. "Are they here?" he asked, tugging at his mother's skirt. Sheyna answered, pulling him close. "Shah, shah, be still. Be patient."

Sarah and Molly were more responsive to the ferry's docking and noticed a couple of the men they had seen at the ship's office earlier making their way to the ferry station.

"They should know something," Sarah said. "It looks like people from the S. S. Netherlands all right." They excused themselves and, without a word, walked briskly toward the ferry.

The people departing the ferry looked prosperous or, at least, comfortably situated. It quickly became clear these were first and second class passengers. Overhearing their conversations, Sarah and Molly judged they were Americans returned from trips abroad or well to do visitors from the Continent. They knew such persons did not have to go through the time consuming process of immigrant inspections and inquiries, only showing their documents at Ellis Island and going directly to the ferries that took them to the city. Hardly any of them were being met. Some had private vehicles with chauffeurs waiting for them.

A gentleman in a dark blue suit with a ship line badge on his jacket carried a briefcase and was heading quickly toward the registry office. Sarah and Molly walked quickly to intercept him.

"Pardon me, Sir. How long before the steerage passengers arrive?" Sarah asked.

Slightly annoyed at the interruption, he snapped, "It shouldn't be too long." Then, he composed himself and added, with a tip of his cap, "But we may have a slight delay. The Captain told me it was a rough trip, with some storms and a few casualties. Be patient. Your people will arrive soon."

The women went back to the waiting benches, anxiety showing on their faces. "This is nerve wracking," said Molly. It was mid afternoon. A half hour later they spotted another ferry coming toward the dock.

This time they recognized steerage passengers by their dress and satchels and bundles of goods. Most of those who had been waiting were crowded near the plank where the passengers exited. The departing immigrants gawked at the huge city skyline and the immensity of the port. They smiled broadly at the reception they received.

From time to time, relatives on shore called out to an arriving immigrant, "Hubert, look over here" or "Shmuel, I'm over here with Anna" or something of the sort. The reunion began with hugs and kisses. Children, in particular, were greeted with affection and comments such as, "Look how much you've grown!" It was a joyous occasion.

Sarah's eyes kept searching the face of each arrival for the appearance of Julius. There was no sight of him, but another ferry was coming right behind the first, so she and Molly moved in that direction. They positioned themselves on a railing so they could see everyone coming from either ferry. Sarah and Molly clasped hands and prepared themselves to jump for joy at the sight of Julius.

The immigrants departed in double lines, but Julius was nowhere to be seen. Sarah stopped a family as they came off one of the ferries, recognizing their dress as typical of Polish Jews, and asked in her best Yiddish, "Do you know of Julius Newman? Was he traveling with you?" She repeated the questions to several of the new arrivals, but in return all she got was shaking of the heads or shrugs.

While she was asking, another official in a similar blue suit and badge descended from the stairway leading from the ferry control cabin and hurried past the throngs toward the old brick building. Sarah and Molly caught up with him.

"Please, Sir," Sarah said pleadingly, "I can't find my brother. Would you check to see if Julius Newman was aboard? Or if he's being kept for some reason at Ellis Island?"

Irving Goetz came looking for someone official to speak with. "Mister, we've been waiting for our cousins, Abraham Solomon and Rivka Borchowitz. Can you help us find them?" His family had joined him.

Sarah turned to Irving. "Oh, so you can't find *them* either."

The ship's agent hesitated and then spoke brusquely. "Some people are being detained but I don't know who they are.

"Another thing, there were some unfortunate incidents on board. If you don't see your relatives, you can ask about them inside," he said. "Those names sound familiar but I can't confirm anything. Yes, someone inside here can tell you more." He abruptly turned and entered the building.

Sarah, Molly, and the Goetzes went back together to the ferries. After they had again searched every face, they returned to the building. Tenseness showed on Sarah's face as she approached the desk clerk. Molly stayed close to Sarah but extended her hand to Sheyna.

Sarah spoke for everyone. She gave the names of all three family members. "What can you tell us about them?" she asked searchingly. "Is there a problem? Maybe we can help if it's more identification they need."

The ship's agent with whom they had spoken outside drew the clerk aside and whispered something in his ear. When the clerk returned, he asked them to sit down. His face was drawn. He had trouble expressing the words.

Finally, he spoke. "There may be some bad news for you. We have it that your three people were reported as 'died on board.' It still needs to be confirmed.

"Died on board?" questioned Sarah, unbelievingly.

"What are you saying?" added Sheyna. "It can't be. They were young and healthy. They were fine when they left Europe. What happened? No, no, that can't be right." She put both hands over her mouth to muffle a shriek.

"I don't know any more about it," replied the clerk. "The Captain. He's the one you have to talk to, and he's already left."

"Usually we don't tell people where he stays, but the boss says you need to talk with him. He's the only one who can tell you about it. I'll write down his address. He went to the Hotel Esplanade on 24th Street near

Eighth Avenue. His name is Captain Harald Meergossen. Go see him. Tell him the ship's agent sent you. We'll try to get word to him to expect you."

Sarah and Molly held on to each other in deep shock, their reserve evaporating under the strain of the news. Sheyna was on the verge of collapse. She kept shaking her head as if that would wipe away what they had just heard. Tears were rolling off Irving's cheeks. Joshua and Charlie, seeing their brother cry, joined in. Sarah was the only one who had not yet begun to cry. The full impact of the clerk's report had not yet sunk in.

Turning toward the clerk, Sarah exclaimed, "There must be a mistake," Sheyna added, "It can't be, it can't be." Her children were clinging to her. Molly, in despair herself, sat at Sheyna's side and tried to comfort her.

Sarah asked again, "Ain't there something more you can tell us?" The Irish clerk pursed his lips, "I'm very, very sorry. Go see the Captain and find out what happened. May God go with you!"

"How horrible if it's really true," Sarah exclaimed, as she finally broke into tears. "Maybe there's a mistake and that's not what happened," she said sobbingly.

Then, gathering herself together and realizing she was the one who had to take charge, she mused, "What can I tell my parents? They expect me to come home with Julius, and what can I say if I go home alone?" She began to tremble at the thought.

Sarah composed herself. She made sure Mrs. Goetz was able to leave and that Irving could get her and his brothers home safely. They exchanged addresses. Sarah told her she will call on her soon. First, she must break the news at home. They will go to see the Captain that day.

Sarah and Molly hardly spoke as they walked toward the streetcar, which got them to within a couple of blocks of the Newmans' apartment. After being seated, Sarah rested her head on Molly's shoulder. Sobbingly, she said, "I still don't believe it. Poor Momma and Poppa, how can I tell them?"

Other passengers on the streetcar looked over to the women, feeling sympathy even if they didn't know what the source of concern was. An elderly woman came over and offered her handkerchief. Sarah and Molly finally left the streetcar. Leaning against each other, they walked the last few blocks slowly to the Newmans' home.

Filled with trepidation, Sarah opened the front door. Mrs. Newman saw the two of them come in. At first she thought they were hiding Julius for a surprise, and she laughed. "So where is he?" she asked, as if playing along with the joke. When she saw the look on Sarah's face, she knew something was not right.

"Tell me," she demanded, her voice rising, "what's wrong?"

Sarah quickly related what she had heard from the people at the boat company. She followed it with "Momma, why has this happened to us?"

Mrs. Newman fell back into an upholstered chair. "Maybe they confused him with someone else," she cried out. "Maybe he missed the boat and he's still in Boulogne or in Poland." She covered her face with her hands.

"No, no, Momma," said Sarah tearfully. "We know he left Poland and boarded the ship for America." Molly slipped into the kitchen to boil some water for tea.

"We need to get more information about what actually happened. I'm going to see the ship Captain. There are two others who were also reported as dying on the ship, Momma. A Mrs. Goetz from near here was related to both of them, and she's going with me to see the Captain."

"Momma, all we can do now is pray that we'll get better news. At least, we can find out what really happened to Julius."

Just then, Mr. Newman arrived home for his promised lunch break from his job at a pharmacy. He saw the stunned look on everyone's face. "Where is my boy?' he asked with a tone of curiosity in his voice. "Julius didn't have any problems at the inspection station, did he?"

"Poppa, the news is not good," said Sarah, her face somewhat contorted. As Mr. Newman grabbed the back of a chair for support, she repeated the story for him. "*Got in himel!*, he cried out. Sarah ran to her father and embraced him as tears rolled freely among all of them.

Amid sobs, Sarah's mother said, "The other night I had a dream something bad had happened to Julius, but I didn't want to tell anyone. That man whose face I saw on the ship when we came over—*ayin horeh*. I kept seeing that face in my dream. I knew it would mean trouble. Now it really has happened. Why should our family suffer like this—in *America?*"

She motioned for Sarah to come over to her. When Sarah went to her, she threw her arms around her and clung to her. "Our family, our family," she wept softly. "That is what we live for. Now we are one less." Sarah buried her head in her mother's arms and wept with her.

Several blocks away, the relatives of Abraham Solomon and Rivka Borchowitz were going through a similar trauma. "Why them?" asked Irving. "How did they die, Momma?" questioned Joshua, frightened at the thought. "I already arranged for Abe to have a job in my factory," said Sheyna's husband, Moishe, whom one of the children had fetched from his work when they got home. *Mein Got!* We need to know what happened."

"Just think," said Sarah, "three people could hardly wait to get to America and enjoy life like us. Now, they're gone. Our Julius and their Abraham and Rivka. What happened to their dream?"

CHAPTER 3

▼

(In the old country before the voyage)

In his village of Kraglova in the Russian Pale of Settlement, Isak Solomon was a tailor with a good reputation. He made clothes for the common folk. More importantly, he was also the tailor for a Russian count who lived on an estate several kilometers away.

Each year, Isak spent extended periods of time at the estate, measuring and fitting the count's family for their finest clothes. Because he often slept at the estate for a night or two at a time, his sons would sometimes accompany him. One helped with the tailoring. The others tended to the cattle and generally helped to maintain the grounds of the estate.

A Jewish tailor serving a Russian Orthodox count was an honor, and Isak earned a handsome amount. It was enough to provide a decent life for his family. With his wife, Taube, he had raised six children—four boys and two girls. Life was still difficult for Isak's family because of the oppressive regimes that governed the Pale. Not even the count could halt the attacks unleashed by the Czar's militia.

The Jews were the scapegoats for nearly everything that went wrong in the area. If the economy was depressed, the government blamed the Jews. When a storm destroyed several houses, the peasants held the Jews responsible. If a disease spread throughout the community, a finger was pointed at them.

The Jews paid a price for these believed wrongdoings. It was not only the limitations placed on work opportunities, and the lack of freedom to move about. There were burdensome taxes on every activity from buying goods to occupying a small piece of land to making animal meat kosher. And there was also the threat of physical harm. At the whim of the Czar and his local agents, raids on Kraglova were frequent. Businesses were sometimes ravaged, houses were burned, and women and children were violated or beaten.

His people had suffered so much, Isak thought to himself. He often wondered why their prayers were not answered. He believed it can only be that Jews hold a special place in the kingdom of God. In His wisdom, God must hold Jews up as an example of the people who turned the other cheek in order to survive and contribute to humanity.

Isak was more concerned about his family than himself. When he was at the count's estate, he could not protect his wife and children at home. He relied on his neighbors to look after them while he was gone.

"My dear Taube," he often said, "be vigilant and make sure the children do not cross paths with those who would harm our loved ones."

Little did he realize how vulnerable *he* was.

Isak had traveled between the Count's estate and his home many times. Occasionally, he would pass Cossacks on horseback. They were never cordial, but they always waved him on.

In the spring of 1862, on a trip back from the estate, he failed to notice a regiment of militia on the road ahead of him until he was in their midst. They stopped and questioned him. He showed his papers and told them who he worked for. When he was commanded to step down from his cart, he did so, but too slowly for the satisfaction of one of the soldiers, who hit Isak with a rifle butt. When he cried out, he was struck several more times and left on the road to die.

When Isak was killed, the family was devastated. After his burial, Taube and five of the children, fearing further attacks, packed some of their goods and left home within days of Isak's death. Only Abraham, the oldest boy, remained in Kraglova. It was a tearful departure. Taube begged Abraham to go with them but he felt it was his duty to maintain the family home.

A sympathetic Christian neighbor hid Taube and the childen in a wagon and brought them to a section of a forest where they could sleep without being noticed. The following night, Taube and the two youngest children safely crossed the border of their province and sought refuge in an adjoining part of the Pale. They were never heard from again.

The three older children took a different route, heading for the Baltic coast. They hoped to make their way to South Africa, where they had relatives. Their fate was also unknown.

Abe was resourceful, like his father. He loved his village. He believed that his roots were there and that was where he should remain. A compassionate man, he loved his family but also was generous to his neighbors. He was a diligent worker.

Abe had learned his father's trade, sitting at Isak's side while he pedaled his sewing machine or hand stitched clothes. He had often assisted his father at the count's estate.

After Isak's death, the count approached Abe and consoled him. "Your father prepared you well for tailoring," he said. "I want you to continue in his place." Abe knew he did not yet have his father's tailoring skills, but he was determined to work hard to satisfy the count. "It would be a great honor, your lordship," he replied. "I am grateful for your confidence."

Abe missed his family life. True, he knew many of the villagers; but they weren't family. His uncles, aunts, and cousins lived in other villages. Working so hard left him little time to travel to them.

Abraham wanted to marry to regain the intimacy of family life. Spending so much time at work left little time for socializing. The fact was he stayed to himself most of the time.

In an effort to meet more available women, he remained at the synagogue after Sabbath services to talk with his neighbors. When synagogue members invited him to dinner, he accepted gladly rather than inventing excuses for not going. His social life improved, but no unmarried woman he met fitted his image of a desirable wife.

Then one day, he went to acquire some fabric and thread from Ber Davidoff, who had provided for Abe's father as well as himself.

As he approached the Davidoff house, that adjoined the family's mill, Abe saw Ber's daughter Bessie working in the garden. She was regarded as the village beauty, and many young men in the village tried to court her. But Bessie liked her independence. She knew she could find a husband very easily, but chose to enjoy single life before becoming a husband's servant.

Abe greeted Bessie timidly. He liked her, of course, but thought "Why would she be interested in an unexciting fellow like me?"

On seeing Abe, Bessie tossed away her gardening tools, wiped her hands on her smock, and extended her hand. Abe quickened his step and reached out to grasp it. He felt his face becoming flushed and could barely offer a greeting. Bessie's smile put him at ease.

"Abe, we sympathize with you in the loss of your father, may he rest in peace, and the disappearance of your family. It must be very difficult for you. Yet, maybe you keep too much inside you. When you have finished with your business, please stay and have some tea."

Her comments confused him but strangely excited him. He was always smitten with Bessie's appearance and gentle ways but had no hope of courting her. His confidence in himself was enhanced. He realized he might possibly become her suitor.

Abe began to visit Bessie weekly. She invited him to tea, talked with him about their neighbors, and showed him her collection of dolls. He told her how important her father had been to the village, what a strange person the sexton at the synagogue was, and how much he enjoyed reading poetry. They laughed together and exulted in each other's company.

Abe had discovered a new outlook on life. Bessie told her parents she had found a man she was in love with.

As they picnicked beside the lake one afternoon, Abe told Bessie he would ask her father for permission to marry her. Bessie was delighted. The two began to plan their future. "Four children would be perfect, maybe even five" said Bessie. "Maybe my business could be joined with your father's," said Abe. "What could be closer than cloth and tailoring?" "Should we live in your place, or should we consider a place closer to where my parents live?" Bessie added. These and other questions filled hours of conversation, and they found they could differ on the answers while still agreeing to face them together.

The Davidoffs were elated with their prospective son in law. They consulted the rabbi and other officials to make plans for the marriage. Bessie and Abe had a joyful wedding attended by friends and relatives from several *shtetls* in the Pale. Aunts and uncles and cousins from both sides attended. The absence of his immediate family preyed on Abe's mind, but an uncle from a nearby village stood in as his best man.

The Jews of Kraglova had never seen such a celebration! The crowd was so large that the wedding canopy had to be squeezed into the bimah. After Abe punctuated the ceremony by smashing a wrapped wineglass with his foot, the crowd surged outside where platters filled with every imaginable food were waiting to be enjoyed. Singing and dancing, led by the bride and groom, and tributes to the betrothed by leaders of the community, highlighted the celebration.

Bessie and Abe's marriage seemed made in heaven. They were constant companions. While Abe worked at his tailoring, Bessie was at his side doing her sewing or reading a book.

But only months after their marriage, before the glow of the wedding could subside, Bessie developed a troubling, persistent cough. Every natural remedy had no effect. When the doctor was called in at last, he quickly recognized tuberculosis and recommended rest and mountain area. Before a move could be arranged, complications set in and her illness became worse.

Watching his wife's decline was gut wrenching for Abe. He remained by her side, neglecting his work. He tended to her every need. He prayed to God, both at home and in synagogue, to spare her life. Within a matter of weeks, however, she was gone.

For Abe, it was a double blow. His dear Bessie was no longer with him and they had conceived no children. To make matters worse, the economy of the area was slumping and Abe's income was no longer as substantial as it had been. The count reduced the amount he paid him, and fewer of the villagers were buying his clothes.

The village rabbi counseled him, "One life is gone but yours remains. You are still young and you will eventually find another wife and have children."

Abe was twenty four when Bessie died. As time went on, he became more strongly committed to his tailoring work, but again the absence of family life made him lonely. He joined friends from time to time to play cards and share a meal, and he wandered by himself through the countryside to observe the joys of nature. The exuberance he had displayed while courting and marrying Bessie had disappeared.

Because most of his work was done while sitting and he exercised very little, Abe grew even more portly. He was not fat; rather, he was solid but with an expanding waistline.

On occasion, he mumbled to himself, "Sit, sit, sit is all I do. It's not good. I have to find a way to lose weight or else I will spend more time making clothes for myself than for others."

Two decades passed with Abe continuing in his daily routines. He had become the premier tailor in Kraglova. After the Count died ten years earlier, Abe had built up his business by catering mostly to the merchants of the town.

Seeing the butcher, Slonim, and the doctor, Steinberg, at Saturday Sabbath services in the well groomed outfits he stitched made his chest swell with pride. At the synagogue, a less well off neighbor commented, "Here I am in rags. So why can't I have one of Abe's suits too? If only I could afford one." Overhearing this remark, Abe showed his generosity by refitting one of his old suits for the neighbor. Even the better off Christians were apt to be wearing Abe's tailored clothes at church on Sunday.

However, Abe was sensitive to the changes going on in his community. More and more of the Jewish villagers were leaving to go to England or the United States. It seemed unlikely that he would find another suitable woman in his *shtetl* to marry. He had gotten encouragement from friends and neighbors. Over the years, the local marriage broker suggested prospects, but nothing materialized. To complicate matters, it was getting harder to manage his small business by himself.

He had never heard from his mother, nor brothers and sisters. "They must have been caught and imprisoned or died," he surmised. "If they were alive, I would have heard some news." He was long past grieving for his family, and had begun to feel sorry for himself. He was now questioning his life.

Abe was not overtly religious; yet he went to Saturday services with regularity and, with the help of neighbors, kept a kosher home. He realized that was not enough.

"My prayers to God are not always answered, that's true," he told a neighbor, "but I am still here on earth so He must have a purpose for me."

"After all," he said, "even if I now earn less than before, I only have myself to take care of. I have my strength. My health is generally good. How can I complain?"

In 1893, Abe had reached age 45. Many of his neighbors were leaving for America. The loneliness that he felt after Bessie died had peaked again.

Life in the village was getting harder. The Czarist regime had increased their vengeance on the Jews. Twice in two months the Cossacks had stormed the town. They beat the villagers and even killed some of the older, more vulnerable ones. They looted and burned homes and one of Abe's customers asked him, "How much can a person take?" Abe shrugged and replied, "Our people have suffered like this for generations."

Abe tried to be reasonable, but his patience was exhausted and he now saw no future staying in the *shtetl*. He wanted a better life than he could have in Kraglova. Moreover, he said to himself, "I always considered myself brave, but honestly I am now afraid for all of us here." Although he had not suffered personally from the evils perpetrated by the Czar's military, he remembered his father. "It will happen to me sooner or later."

CHAPTER 4

▼

Abe's relatives lived in the village of Blutz, about 25 kilometers from Kraglova. He heard from his Uncle Eliezer, who had stood for him at his wedding to Bessie, that his cousins had left for America. Abe wrote to his cousins who had crossed the Atlantic. He thought perhaps he might finally have news about the fate of his family.

Abe's second cousin, Lazer Solomon, had been in America for three years. He was a clothing stitcher in a small factory that made ladies garments. Lazer marveled at how good life was in the new land. "It's not perfect," he wrote to Abe, "but there is freedom here and a chance for a good life."

Another second cousin, Sheyna, who had married a Goetz from Riga and had three sons, kept a steady flow of letters coming to him. She begged Abe to join them. Abraham Solomon was becoming convinced that leaving was desirable.

Still, he wanted to be absolutely sure he would not be making a mistake. He felt he needed to talk personally with people he had confidence in. So he arranged to drive his horse and cart to Blutz. The place was not the size of Kraglova and off the main roads of the Pale, but its market drew people from the outlying rural areas. Being somewhat off the beaten track, it was not a major target for Cossack attacks.

Abe wrote to Uncle Eliezer:

"If it meets with your approval, I plan on visiting you a week from Tuesday. You have been like a father to me. Now, I need a father's advice. Business is not so good. I have to admit that I am not happy. Relatives write that I should go to America. My head is all mixed up, like tsimmes."

The visit was thus arranged, and Abe set off for Blutz. In those days and in that part of the world, traveling 25 kilometers in a horse and cart was no pleasant outing. This horse was a good companion. In their seven years together, they had traveled together many times. On longer trips, Abe even found himself talking to it.

The trip was arduous for both of them with several stops for watering and occasional rests for both Abe and the horse. The roads were full of potholes and rocks, and it was tiring to maneuver the cart around them.

Even though it was early spring, there were still pockets of snow and ice from the winter storms in ditches and ravines. Abe started out early in the morning to make certain he would arrive in Blutz before sundown.

He worried when one of the wheels started to wobble, but he slowed down and was extra careful.

As he neared Blutz, he saw people he knew and exchanged a few words with them.

"How are the children?" he asked a woman planting spring vegetables.

"Fine, fine," she answered. "I haven't seen you for a while."

"Have the terrorists bothered you lately?" he inquired of an elderly man he had once met at his cousin's house.

"Only once this month."

"May God give us strength to carry on in this horrible environment," Abe replied.

On arriving at his uncle's home, he secured his cart and comforted the horse. When Uncle Eliezer and Aunt Dora came out to meet him, he embraced them with gusto.

"You have room for me to stay tonight?" Abe asked his short, stocky aunt. "Don't worry," she replied. "Should we turn away our favorite nephew?" Broad smiles were on all the faces.

They ushered him into the kitchen. "Here, here," said Dora. "I just baked these cakes this morning. They are nice and fresh." They exchanged news and pleasantries. Abe sipped his tea, but he had important matters to discuss and not much time to waste. He nodded toward Eliezer as a sign that they had to get about their business.

Eliezer, a younger brother of Abe's father, was in his sixties. He was much taller than Isak, probably close to six feet. Graying hair surrounded a bald spot in the middle of his head, and a short beard ran from ear to ear. He had often visited Isak and Taube and loved the children. After Isak's death and disappearance of the rest of the family, he and Abe exchanged letters and visited occasionally. The last time Eliezer came to Kraglova, Abe had made his uncle a suit to wear at Sabbath services.

Though Eliezer longed for a better existence elsewhere, his *shtetl* was his home and he couldn't face leaving. Yet, he understood quite well why others left and he assisted them in ways he could.

Acknowledging Abe's nod, Eliezer motioned toward another room and told Dora they had things they needed to talk about. Moving to a porch on the other side of the house, they settled in chairs across from each other.

"I don't know what future there is for any of us here, Abe, but the Good Lord will take care of us in His own way," said the uncle. "As for you, going to America is not a bad idea. Also, living alone is not good. You need a wife who can give you love and companionship.

"I'm surprised you haven't picked a wife already. Bessie was an angel, but she is gone. She would have wanted you to marry again. Abe, you have plenty of attractive girls among your relatives and acquaintances, both here and elsewhere. You should choose one of them for a bride and have a new start.

"You remember your sister Esther's friend, Rachel? She lives not far away, and I understand she isn't married yet. Her parents are looking for a husband for her.

"And what about your cousin Rivka? She lives close by. What a lovely woman! You've seen her many times, so you know what I mean. She's maybe five or six years younger than you."

"Of course, you're right," sighed Abe pensively, "but I'm not entirely convinced I can make a living in America. If I can work on my own, maybe that would be all right. But, if I have to work for someone else, in a factory for example, I just don't know. It will take a lot of adjustment."

Eliezer responded, "You have to have confidence. Others before you have made it and even done well. You'll have family and friends in America. God seems to be telling us there are better lands and we should go and find them and settle there.

"For me, things haven't been all that bad. Who knows what the future holds, but for now Dora and I can stay here. For you, on the other hand, there seems to be no alternative. If you stay where you are, you will risk your father's fate.

"The time is right for you to pack up and head for the United States, or even South Africa. You might discover some of your lost family there." With that comment, Eliezer leaned back and nodded as if he was urging Abe to agree with him.

"What we all go through in the Pale is devastating," Abe said with some anger in his voice. "I don't like the idea of leaving my neighbors and relatives; but, increasingly, they are leaving me. You're right. For my sanity if not my life, I must go somewhere else to start over again.

"As for my family, who knows where they are now. My searches over the years have turned up nothing. Maybe they *are* in South Africa, maybe Italy, maybe even America. My conscience certainly hurts at not having seen my dear mother for so many years. God knows how it's pained me. Is she alive or dead? I don't know. As for my brothers and sisters, I don't know either.

"If I go to another country, it must be to a place where I know there are friends. Right now, that's the United States. Of course, having someone alongside me would make a difference. It's been a while since I've seen Rivka, probably four or five years. I think it was at a bar mitzvah in Kraglova. Do you really think she would be interested in me?"

Eliezer raised his head and, with a smile, looked directly at Abe. "You think that was an idle thought when I mentioned Rivka? Ha, ha!" he laughed heartily.

"For a long time now, many of us have said what a good match that would be, you and Rivka. For a long time, we didn't say anything. We figured you'd realize it yourself. I'm sure that Rivka's family has had the same thought from time to time. Look, have a good night's rest here and in the morning we'll go over to the Borchowitz place. It would be good just to renew acquaintance, even if nothing happens from it."

He smiled broadly, "But a little birdie tells me you and Rivka will have a meeting of minds. Her family will be thrilled. Besides, Rivka has talked of going to America."

Later that night, Abe could not fall asleep. His mind kept straying from one part of his conversation with Eliezer to another. "Rivka, why didn't I think of her?" he thought to himself. Soon, though, his mind became foggy. The trip had taken a lot out of him and he was tired. He fell into a deep sleep.

CHAPTER 5

▼

Early the following morning, Abe awakened to the sounds of chickens clucking and mules braying. As he glanced through the only window in the room, he noticed birds flying from one corner of the roof to another as they greeted the morning.

Uncle Eliezer was already up and tending to his chores. Aunt Dora was preparing breakfast. Abe came in quietly and his aunt greeted him with "Good morning. I hope you slept well."

"Good morning, good morning," replied Abe. "Oh, was I tired. I hope my snoring didn't wake you up."

"I didn't hear it," said Dora, "but maybe I was snoring at the same time." They both chuckled, and Abe stretched.

Eliezer came in from the barn. "You're up—and feeling rested, I presume. We're all hooked up and ready to go. Finish your breakfast, and then we can be on our way. Podblutz is only a short distance."

Heading down the road, Eliezer and Abe engaged in idle banter. The uncle told stories about different pieces of land they passed and some of their occupants.

"That one over there, the family was arguing about leaving for America. Some said yes, some said no. It's usually the older people who want to stay. Eventually, the younger ones will go, and maybe the older ones will come later. If a father has a job waiting for him in America, he will go first and the rest of the family will join him when he's found a place for them."

Further down the road, he remarked, "Now, here is a sad story. Just when everything was going fine, the father's heart gives out and his wife and children don't know what to do. They were all dependent on him."

He also told about cousin Israel Borchowitz's place, in a nearby rural area with a patch of land for crops out back. "The government several years ago told Jews they couldn't be in farming any more. They didn't want competition for the Russian farmers. They wanted Jews to live in the villages so they could control their homes and work."

"But they made an exception in Israel's case, because he had been there for so long and he was well liked by his neighbors."

Abe listened, but his mind wasn't exactly tuned into his uncle's chatter. He was thinking of Rivka and how he would approach her.

"What should I say? How should I act? What if she shows no interest in me? Are there other men who would be competing for her hand?"

Ever since Bessie died, twenty years earlier, he had denied himself the close affection of women. He almost felt guilty at the thought of replacing her. But, if he was to form a new loving relationship with Rivka or another woman, he would have to learn how to act as a husband all over again.

Soon, the Borchowitz house loomed into view. It was a small wooden structure with a flat roof covered with a thick layer of straw and sat close to the road. Eliezer drove his cart to the front and stopped. A parcel of land, no more than five acres, stood in back of the house and Israel could be seen working in the field.

When Israel saw the cart arrive, he made his way quickly to the house. About the same time, his youngest daughter, Yetta, came out the front door to greet the guests. Her long black skirt was covered with a hand-made apron stitched across the middle with flowers.

"Good day, Cousin Eliezer," Yetta called out. "And Cousin Abe, too." She was the picture of her mother as Abe had remembered her from years ago—a bit short and a bit stout, with a broad smile on her face. She glanced back at her father, who had now come within talking distance. He had a slight limp, due to a farming accident, and one of his eyes was half closed because of an injury from when he was a young man.

Since Israel's wife, Beila, had become ill several years before, Yetta was now performing many of the household chores. All the children, except for Yetta and Rivka, were married and living in adjoining communities.

"Hello, hello." Israel called out. "It's so good to see you. At least you're not the tax collector." He kept a straight face, while the others laughed. He was always one to make jokes, even when things looked grim.

"So, to what do we owe the pleasure of a visit? Maybe you've brought me some money or jewels. Or is it that you'll give me an invitation from Czar Alexander III to attend his next family gathering?"

"How did you guess?" replied Eliezer, grinning. "We're all invited by the Czar. Get dressed in your best clothes. We have to leave soon to get to the palace on time."

He continued, "So why shouldn't relatives see more of each other? We've been too much living apart and not enjoying each other's company. Abe hasn't been here for a long time and we agreed it would be nice to stop by." Yetta nodded her head.

"How is Beila? I hope her health has improved."

"As God is my witness," Israel said, "she looks much better today than she has in quite a while. She must have known you were coming. Let's go inside and you can judge for yourselves."

The four of them went into the house where Beila was resting in an overstuffed chair. "Beila, we have guests, our rich cousins," Israel said, with the same dry humor. "Stay in your chair. They'll come to you."

Eliezer called out, "We're not so rich with money, but we have a wealth of good heart."

Beila was pale and thinner than when Eliezer had last seen her. But she smiled and motioned for her guests to sit with a wave of her hand.

"You remember cousin Abe Solomon, of course," Eliezer said.

"Of course."

"He hasn't been here for some time," Eliezer continued. "Abe is thinking of going to America. Such thinking we all should do, but not all of us can manage it right now."

"Come have something to drink, some cake maybe," invited Yetta. "It's my special pound cake."

The door to an adjoining room opened and Rivka appeared, carrying a piece of needlework. She spent much of her day sewing for a dressmaker. The Singer hand driven sewing machine she used was their family treasure. The meager pay Rivka earned helped the family's budget and gave her a few rubles for her own use.

Abe's eyes were fixed on Rivka. He remembered seeing her first as a small girl and recalled her presence at his wedding to Bessie. She was a young lady then, charming but not a beauty. They had met a few times since then, but not for several years now.

Rivka, now in her late thirties, was stunning. Her long brown hair was tied up into a ball on top of her head. Her deep brown eyes were radiant. An apron accentuated an hour glass figure. She carried herself well and revealed dimpled cheeks when she smiled.

"Rivka, it's good to see you. It's been a few years," he said, rising from his chair. "Time passes by so quickly. I almost didn't recognize you." He leaned over to kiss her hand. Other family members broke into broad grins.

"Abe, I remember you well," said Rivka, "and your wedding. What a great occasion—the ceremony, having all the family together. It was a terrible loss, your Bessie."

"Yes, she certainly was a fine woman. I shall never forget her. But it's been many years since then. I've put that part of my life behind me."

"The last time I spoke to you was at little Mozel's bar mitzvah," Rivka added, as they moved to a corner of the room. "The gathering afterward was so crowded. I don't think we had a chance to say more than a few words to each other. Yes, time flies. Mozel is already in military service.

"What brings you here today?"

The others were in conversations among themselves.

Adjusting his jacket and appearing self conscious, Abe looked directly in Rivka's eyes and said in a whisper, "Oh, I am so much to myself these days. I thought I should talk to my relatives. I first went to Eliezer and he suggested this visit. I've been thinking about the future and what it will bring. My business is not doing so well. The troubles affecting our people are becoming more and more unbearable.

"The future. Who can make plans with so many uncertainties? I get an idea and then drop it. I get another idea and then forget about it. But I listen to people and I exchange letters with some friends and relatives. So, finally, I think I now have an idea I can stick with.

"What it comes down to is that I've decided to go to America sometime soon. I'm told there are good jobs there and a free life we've never had here. A lot of our people have already made the move. I hear good things from some of them, like our cousin Sheyna. She's one of them."

At that point, Rivka suggested they walk out to the porch, where they would have more privacy. "We're going to step outside for a minute," she called to her parents. Eliezer looked up and nodded approvingly.

Once seated on the porch, Rivka went on. "Of course, we all think about going to America. It's so hard for my parents to be serious about it now, with my mother so sick. She couldn't survive the voyage. But I've also made up my mind to go to the United States. I want to get established there and arrange for the others to join me later. God willing, Mama's health will improve.

"I haven't figured out all the details yet, but I am going."

Abe cut in quickly, "You will go by yourself, or others will go with you? People will meet me in New York, but on the trip I will be by myself."

Rivka threw a cotton wrap around her shoulders because of a chill outside. "I've also heard from our cousins there and they're anxious for me to come. My good friend, Anna Jacobsohn from Bialystok, is going to America, too. We have written letters and discussed our plans. It would be nice to be companions on the trip.

"Most people from Blutz go to Hamburg to get a ship for America. I hear you can leave from Bremen or Libau, too. A shipping line agent came to Blutz two weeks ago to talk to people. He can make the arrangements. He said the cost was 15 American dollars for third class."

"Maybe it's the same fellow who came to our village," said Abe. "He books your passage on a ship, but getting to the ship is the traveler's problem. I've discussed it with people whose families have gone recently. You need official papers and a passport. The authorities aren't cooperative where Jews are concerned. If they don't turn you down, they delay your papers.

"The first problem is getting out of the Pale. After that, you can go the rest of the way. It can take a long time, though, and there are police and border agents to get by.

"The shipping line agents gave us the names of people who can create papers for you, and also who can see that you are met by different people along the way. A night here, a night there. There are many hurdles to getting to the ship before it sails. Others have done it, though, and I expect to do it too."

Abe straightened up in his chair and looked at Rivka. "Maybe you can go with me. I've heard that ships now sail for America from Holland. And that the wait for a ship is not as long as from Hamburg. What do you think?"

"I hadn't heard about that. It seems like you've investigated the situation thoroughly. What would it take for both of us to go on the same ship? I mean—can the agent make bookings for both of us? It's something to think about.

"Of course, we probably shouldn't travel together from here. An unmarried woman and a man traveling together can raise many eyebrows. The authorities could punish us if our papers are not exactly right. Besides, I promised Anna Jacobsohn to travel with her. I should hear from her this week about her plans."

Abe stood up, took a few steps, and then sat back down. He nodded his head a few times without speaking. He glanced at her, turned his head away, and then looked back at her again. He then mustered the courage to speak.

"I understand what you're saying. But you know, Rivka—excuse me for being so forward—but many people have told me what a wonderful wife you would make." His face turned a bit red. "From seeing you again, I agree completely. You may not see much in me, but I can provide for you."

Abe moved about uneasily in his chair. "My heart is even racing as we speak, Rivka. What I mean to say is we should think about the possibility of getting married. If not in this country, then when we get to America.

"Going to America can be hard, the strangeness of it all. A married couple can manage better than two who are unmarried. Besides, being with you would give *me* a new life. Rivka, we could be married. What do you think?"

Rivka now smiled and blushed a bit. She looked off to the side. "I've always liked you, Abe, and getting married to you might be what the Lord intends. But let's not rush things. Let's just agree that, if we go to America, either on the same ship or at the same time, we'll get to know each other better. We can then be more certain that marriage is the wise thing to do.

"Abe, this is so sudden. I want to talk with my family. I'm not a young girl whose family has to make a match," she said, looking uncomfortable. "At my age, I can decide things for myself. Yet, I want their approval.

"Abe, after I've talked with everyone I'll send you a letter about plans."

Abe perked up on hearing Rivka's suggestion. "You're an intelligent and practical woman, Rivka. I understand your position. I have to get back to my village today. I'll wait for your letter and then I'll send you the details about the ship to America, about meeting in Holland. You and I can travel together."

Rivka agreed, looking into his eyes and smiling. The two stood up and embraced, more like cousins than a couple planning to be married. They went back into the sitting room.

Israel was still cracking jokes and they were all laughing. Abe and Rivka's return invited probing looks.

"Well," said Eliezer, displaying smugness in having facilitated the meeting, "have you two made application for American citizenship yet?"

"It should only happen for all of us," added Israel.

Abe took Israel aside and explained briefly what he and Rivka had talked about. He looked pleadingly at Israel for his approval. Israel grasped Abe's hands, shook them vigorously, and gave an atypical grin. "I think this was certainly a good visit."

"It's getting late," said Abe. "We should be on our way," he added, glancing in Eliezer's direction. "Could you wrap some cake for me?" he asked Yetta. "I'll eat it on the way home.

Turning to Beila, he said, "May your health return to you quickly."

"What I pray for every day," she said.

To Yetta he remarked, "You are a wonderful daughter to your parents—and such a good baker."

Yetta replied, "It was a joy to see you again, Abe."

To Israel he commented, "May the day come when we will all meet in America."

Embracing Rivka, he said, "We will see each other before too long. Write to me with your plans."

Everyone in the room seemed to be in good spirits. Even Beila had a glow on her face. The rest of them followed Eliezer and Abe outside and wished them well.

The travelers climbed on to the cart. Seeing waves and hearing farewells behind them, they started back down the road.

At Eliezer's, Abe readied his horse and cart for the journey back to his *shtetl*. He hurried to be home before dark. It was not so safe on the road after sunset.

The trip home seemed shorter. Thoughts of Rivka stirred feelings he had pushed down for so many years. He had a lot to do.

The trip to Holland had to be planned for. He needed to arrange for travel. Which belongings should he take with him, and how should he dispose of the things he'd leave behind? He needed to inform friends and neighbors, and alert relatives abroad. Of course, he expected to hear positively from Rivka soon; otherwise, his plans would be different.

He didn't even remember some of the landmarks he passed on the way home. He was tired and the trip was uneventful. As he entered Kraglova, his birthplace, he wondered if it would soon become just a memory. He arrived home just before nightfall, put the horse in the barn, took care of some necessary chores, and hastened to bed.

A few days later he heard from Rivka by messenger. She had accepted the arrangement they had discussed! He was elated. He grabbed a pillow from the sofa and kissed it, imagining the pillow to be Rivka. His first task now was arranging their passage on the same ship.

The following morning, he sought out the agent who had approached him about going to America. "So tell me, friend," he said casually when he saw him in the market square, "I'm going to America. There will be two of us. We hope to sail from Holland for New York. Can you fix it up for us?"

The agent, dressed in wrinkled pants and a moth eaten woolen coat that seemed heavy for the warming weather, flashed a broad grin. "Aha," he said, "I knew you would come to me sooner or later. You can't imagine the number of people I've been making arrangements for. This village, that village, even relatives from distant places. Now almost everybody wants to go. Of course, it's not a simple matter. It will take time and people will have to be paid, but it can be done. Certainly."

CHAPTER 6

▼

Rivka looked at herself in the mirror in the small room she shared with Yetta. "*So Abe thinks I'm pretty.*" She turned side to side, glancing over her shoulder. At times she thought she was, at other times she wasn't so sure.

"That mole on my left cheek. My dry hair. A neck that's too big. Why would any man think I'm attractive? But then who am I to judge?"

Reflecting back to her childhood and since, Rivka's visions of her changing life race through her mind. "*Why have so many bad things happened to me? Here I am thirty nine and still not married.*" Years of helping her father in the fields, bringing him tools he needed, tending the cows, feeding the chickens, had given her a sense of responsibility and tied her closer to her family, but there was not yet a future for her with a family of her own.

As a little girl she had enjoyed life. As children ought, she was unaware of the family's poverty. Her father had a small farm that produced enough for a good day at the market and still left something for the family to eat well. Her mother tended the house and the six children.

Her two brothers went to the synagogue in Blutz with their father and studied the Torah, as was expected of them. They worked on their father's farm whenever they had spare time, and when they grew up they left home. Louis, the older of the boys, became a clerk in a clothing shop in Blutz and later became proprietor when the owner passed away. Isadore managed a farm for some Christians about 25 kilometers from their home and settled full time into agricultural life.

Rivka's sisters were good playmates and good helpers. Fannie and Mariasha, the oldest, assisted their mother in the house and cared for Yetta, the youngest. They all accepted their roles. "*What more is there to life?*" thought Rivka.

She heard that Jews in the towns had more social activities, but they also got more unfavorable attention from authorities. Many had suffered at the hands of the Czar's troops. Her mother and father discussed it over dinner frequently, and the children were sensitive to the plight of their fellow townsmen.

When Rivka was born (in 1855), Europe was emerging from the Industrial Revolution. The Baltic region where she lived had barely been affected by the changes going on, and even the remaining European part of the Russian Empire had not yet fully made the transition.

Alexander II, one of a long line of Russian Czars, came into power about the time of Rivka's birth and ruled for 26 years. It was his Russia the Borchowitz family knew as the children grew up. Because of his popular ideas, Alexander II was known as the "czar liberator." He freed the serfs in Russia, carried out judicial reforms, improved the financial administration, ceased censorship of the press, and permitted provincial representative assemblies. These were all in contrast to the positions his father, the former Czar, had held.

He encouraged industrialization and the building of railroads. But, later in his rule, he found opposition to these developments, mainly from peasants and the new brand of revolutionaries whose thoughts were shaped by Marxian philosophy. The peasants felt agriculture was being denied, and the revolutionaries believed city workers were being abused. In 1881, violent opposition resulted in his assassination.

His son, Alexander III, thought more like his grandfather than his father. A strict authoritarian, he diminished educational programs, strengthened the police system, and persecuted revolutionaries and Jews. He eased the burden of the small farmers but allowed science, music, and literature to flourish during his reign.

His treatment of Jews provided the impetus for the major waves of Jewish emigration to other countries. When the Borchowitzes spoke of the Czar, they were referring to Alexander III.

Occasionally, the Borchowitzes would load up their wagon to visit family members in distant villages. Recollections of some of these visits stuck in Rivka's mind; those not linked to special events faded from her memory.

One trip she did recall was for the wedding of her cousin Abe Solomon. Because Abe's father had died years earlier at the hands of Russian Cossacks, and his mother, brothers, and sisters had disappeared, as many cousins who could come were at his wedding to wish him well. Rivka smiled to herself when she recalled the joyous occasion. The bride was radiant. The family members, happy to be together, were high spirited. The food was grand. Abe and Bessie looked longingly at each other under the *chuppah*. As the musicians played and sung *klezmer* tunes, everyone participated in the traditional dances. They lifted the bride and groom on chairs above their heads and swirled with great joy.

After the wedding, her younger sister Yetta asked Rivka, "When will you have a wedding like that?" Rivka smiled. "That's what I was thinking about all during the ceremony. When I told Momma I wanted to be a bride, too, she told me there was plenty of time for that. "First, enjoy being a young girl,' she said."

At the time, it wasn't so much the beauty of a wedding that interested Rivka as having a suitor. She often spied on her sisters when they were visited by their young men. Fannie and Mariasha kept shooing her and Yetta outside. They complained to their mother, who smiled and said, "One of these days you will want to be alone with your sweethearts."

Rivka was wise beyond her seventeen years. Whenever her father loaded the wagon with vegetables to take to town, she begged to join him. She enjoyed reading, an interest her older brothers and sisters passed along to her. While her father talked to the shopkeepers and other farmers, Rivka devoured everything in print—shop signs, the labels on store goods, the rare newspapers or books. It was her door to the outside world. When she got home, she would tell Yetta as much as she could remember about what she had seen.

The Rabbi's wife sometimes took girls in the community on excursions. In the summer of 1872 she invited Rivka and two other girls to spend a month with her friends in Kovno. Rivka loved the city. She visited the library, where she stayed to read all kinds of books, not just religious ones. She read as many as she could, letting them transport her to faraway places. It was one of her great joys.

Her sisters' romances blossomed into weddings. Sisters Fannie and Mariasha were married in Blutz in a double ceremony. It was a simple ceremony and, befitting the family's economic condition, a modest celebration. The double betrothal brought many families together. Rivka was wide eyed throughout the festivities. She wanted to be next in line to be married and talked excitedly with her mother. Rivka began noticing young men, and several unmarried friends of her of new brothers in law were introduced to her.

Back home, she was attracted to Avram Leib, the eldest son of the town butcher. Seeing him one day when her mother was buying kosher meat and chicken for the week, she struck up a conversation.

"So, Avram, will you be helping to build the *sukkoh* next month?"

"Of course. You'll have to join me in decorating it. It will need a woman's touch."

They both laughed. "Very well," said Rivka, "I'll be sure to be there."

Rivka and Avram began seeing each other whenever they had a chance. She found excuses for going to town whenever someone else was headed that way, and she always "just happened" to bump into Avram at his father's butcher shop. He saw in her a girl who was both pleasant and intelligent. They made small talk and occasionally wandered outside the shop to carry on their conversation.

She looked forward to the Sabbath, when she could catch sight of Avram at the synagogue. Their romance blossomed, and they even joked about "getting ahead of the marriage maker," an elderly woman in the community who was proud of choosing which young men and women should be selected for marriage. One day the old lady said to him, "What's the matter, Avram? You don't like the tailor's daughter I introduced you to? She's just right for you."

One day, Avram told his mother, "You know, Mama, Reb Borchowitz has very good vegetables on his farm. It would be wise to go to the farm and get the first pick of the crops before they're taken to market." His mother listened to him, not sensing his real motive. "You're right. Why don't you get some beets and lettuce. Here are some rubles."

When such trips were made, a little extra time was found for Avram and Rivka to stroll together. They talked about family or neighbors who had left for America or South Africa. At the time, neither of them believed they were destined to leave the area, but the stories they heard about others were interesting and the two of them discussed the advantages and disadvantages of emigrating.

Because Rivka valued her independence, they often talked about roles of men and women. Avram, who was more traditional in his thinking and a 22 year old steeped in Talmudic lessons, told Rivka: "In my family the women are responsible for keeping the house and raising children. But you, dear Rivka, are different from other women. Even without Yeshiva studies, you grasp ideas very well and know about other places and cultures. We hear how times are changing and women want to exercise their minds.

"As for me, I am studying religious matters. I don't give much time to thinking about other things. But I must admit that I, too, have a wandering mind. What I hear about what's going on in the world interests me."

Avram was a scholar, in the sense that he spent most of his time studying the Torah and other Jewish religious writings, as was expected of a son of an important man in the community. But he also helped his father in the butcher shop. There would come a day when he would have to make up his mind as to becoming a rabbi or a butcher. Certainly, a rabbi would have much higher status, but even a butcher was a key element in Jewish life, as a provider of kosher meat in keeping with the dietary laws.

They had talked about the decision he would soon have to make. It didn't matter to Rivka as to what occupation Avram followed. The love they shared and the family they would raise were foremost in her mind.

She knew it was only a matter of time until they would marry. But these matters were not to be hurried. Parents had to be convinced it was completely their idea. Mrs. Borchowitz saw Rivka and Avram together frequently, but it was not the doing of the marriage maker and, according to custom, young people should be guided to matrimony by their elders.

After some months had passed, Rivka's mother confronted her, "I see you are serious about Avram He's a good boy and comes from a good family. Your father and I need to get to know him better."

Mrs. Borchowitz took the kettle from the wood stove and poured hot water over tea leaves in a small earthen pot. She put down two cups and saucers and uncovered a plate of cookies. The two sat down at the table to continue their talk.

"Yes, Momma. Maybe he isn't the best looking young man in town, but he's fun to be with and he has a good mind. We talk about a lot of different things—what it takes to make a good living, the joys of raising a family, and other things." She turned so she was facing her mother more directly.

"Avram knows women should be housewives and raise the children. But he says the world is changing and, after all, it would be a shame not to use my mind for other things. He wants to become a rabbi and serve a synagogue in a city. If we get married, besides keeping house, I will be a rabbi's wife and help him serve the congregation there. That idea excites me, Momma."

"Well, why shouldn't we have him over for dinner? We don't know the family well. For your father and his, a nod or two in the synagogue and a few words after services is about all. I rarely get to speak to Reb Leib in the butcher shop."

"I'll talk to your father about it and, if he approves, you can give him your father's invitation." Rivka beamed and hugged her mother.

A few weeks later, after Avram had been to dinner and impressed the Borchowitzes, Rivka told Yetta the good news. "Things are moving along. Avram's family and ours will be meeting here."

"How wonderful," said Yetta. "I'm so happy for you."

Avram's parents, Heshel and Sore Leib, arrived at the Borchowitz house for dinner. Rivka and Yetta had worked hard to make the house spotless and the silverware glisten. Flowers decorated the table and the sideboards.

Spirits were high. Israel cracked his jokes and Heshel tried to match them. The borscht, roast chicken, and vegetables were consumed, sweets were passed around. Israel led the discussion in his typical jocular vein. "My good friends," he addressed the Leibs, "The Good Lord has arranged something without waiting for the *shadchen*, our village marriage maker." There was laughter all around.

"Our children, Rivka and Avram, make a wonderful match. Now our job is to prepare for a joyous wedding ceremony. I propose we have the wedding here at our house."

Rivka and Avram, on opposite sides of the dining table, glowed and cast glances at each other.

"We can have the ceremony under the grape arbor outside this house. The rabbi from Blutz will conduct the ceremony. We will make all the arrangements."

Heshel Leib accepted the plan. "Let me say to one and all: This marriage is truly being made in heaven. Avram tells me so much what a wonderful person Rivka is that I am wondering if she has hypnotized him." Everyone laughed. "Of course, I say that in jest. Sore and I are delighted to welcome Rivka to our family. And the many children they will have will bring *naches* to us all."

The celebration continued well into the late evening hours, with lively discussions about the wedding arrangements.

Rivka was never happier. Beginning the following day, she spent a lot of time at her sewing machine stitching new clothes and household linens to add to her trousseau. She flitted here and there to discuss wedding plans with her mother and sisters, who had come to help her prepare for the wedding.

One afternoon several days later, the Rabbi from Blutz arrived at the Borchowitz house and, after greeting family members, he whispered something to them. Israel called to Rivka.

She assumed the Rabbi was there to talk about the wedding. He gave a half smile and asked her to sit down.

"My dear Rivka, I regret I have something dreadful to tell you," he said, his lips pursed. "This morning, a group of the Czar's militia stormed into town. They set fire to the synagogue building. Some of the men escaped to their homes, but others were trapped inside and burned. Two men died in the fire."

Rivka's face tensed. "How horrible!" She tried to imagine which of the men in the community had met that awful fate.

"Your Avram stayed behind to help the older men get out of the building. Rivka, pray to God, he was a victim of the fire. He was one of the two who died."

Rivka at first couldn't believe what she was hearing. Then, the impact of the message cut through her like a knife. She shrieked in horror. "No. no." She ran to her bedroom and fell sobbing on the bed. The Rabbi, followed byYetta and her parents, went to console her.

"How terrible!," cried Yetta.

The Rabbi, deeply disturbed, began to elaborate about the scene at the synagogue. "It was mid morning and some of the men were praying; others were in the yeshiva teaching the boys. I was in my office. We heard horses and shouting outside, and before anyone could even get to the door, we saw flames. They spread quickly to the roof and into all the rooms. There was bedlam. We tried to get people out of the building as fast as possible through front doors. A few escaped through the narrow door in the rear. The fire spread so rapidly. The oldest men could not move through the flames. Avram and two other young men went back to help them. In a short time, the fire covered the whole building. It was a tragedy I couldn't have imagined. Several of the men were badly burned. Avram and another young man lost their lives.

"We must have a service and bury Avram's remains at the cemetery before sundown. His family is making the preparations."

Rivka, half listening to the Rabbi, sobbed relentlessly.

The Rabbi continued, "Avram was a brave man. His loss may be great-est for his family and for you, Rivka, but we all feel the emptiness. Now he is in God's service."

In the weeks and months after Avram's death, Rivka withdrew from everything but her sewing work. Her grief was inconsolable. Family, friends, and neighbors tried to comfort her but they could not convince her that this was meant to be and her future would still have many bright spots.

She stopped going into town except when absolutely necessary. In the years that followed, she devoted herself mainly to household duties. She spent endless hours in her room continuing her paid work on the sewing machine. She withdrew from company, even family members. When her family and relatives gathered for a holiday, Rivka made an appearance but remained withdrawn.

The *shadkhan* visited her home from time to time, trying to arrange a meeting for Rivka with a young man here or another one there. All were successful and good looking men, the matchmaker told her.

Occasionally she agreed to meet someone. None compared with Avram. None was a man she wanted to spend the rest of her life with.

One of Rivka's occasional pleasures was taking long walks with Yetta or another sister. They liked to go to a clearing in the woods several kilome-ters from their house. There they sat on a blanket, eating food brought from home and talking about family matters or news from the village.

Rivka might say, "I am concerned about how hard Papa works in the field. I wonder if we shouldn't spend more time helping him. His health is not as good as it was."

Yetta would discuss how she handled her kitchen duties. "I changed Mama's recipe for *borscht* and everyone liked it," she said one time.

Fannie, careful not to bring back bitter memories, told about her hus-band, Al Zeiden, and how they hoped to have children soon.

Sometimes they headed in the direction of Blutz, but after one or two kilometers they felt the need to go back home and tend to chores. The change of scene was good for them and they always met people they knew along the way.

At other times, they sauntered through the woods behind her father's field. Sometimes they followed a small road that went to other farms, most of them run by *goyim*.

Rivka slowly came out of her depression and began to enjoy life a bit more. She caught herself laughing more often and looked forward to her sisters' and brothers' visits.

On one of the walks, she suggested, "Today, let's go as far as the Horstmann place." Yetta giggled and glanced at Rivka, knowing her purpose. It was to see the son of a farmer she had recently met when his father came to the Borchowitz farm. Martin Horstmann was about twenty five, strikingly handsome with blond hair and a strong build. His father, a German Lutheran, became friendly with her father a couple of years earlier.

On most Friday market days, the fathers generally traveled in tandem to the town center. When Mr. Borchowitz was not feeling quite well, or didn't have a sufficient yield to take to market, Martin's father dealt for both of them. They would load the produce onto Mr. Horstmann's wagon before he went into town. In at least one instance the roles were reversed and Mr. Borchowitz became the mutual marketer. The two men had worked out such arrangements when they first collaborated. In exchange for selling his produce, Mr. Borchowitz let his neighbor keep a quarter of the sale money. They trusted each other completely.

From time to time, Martin accompanied his father on the market run. This meant he went to the Borchowitz farm to load up the produce, chickens, eggs and other goods to be sold. Rivka made a point to greet him. The first time, what started out as casual conversation about the weather, turned into more serious talk about their mutual interest—reading.

A relative sent Martin German mystery books which he enjoyed. He pulled one out of a bag on his wagon. "Can you read German?" "Fairly well," replied Rivka. "Here," said Martin, "you can borrow this one, if you'd like."

Sometimes, Martin took walks by himself in the vicinity of the Borchowitz farm. A romance had not yet developed, but he and Rivka enjoyed talking. Martin might say, "It's a shame you have to follow Jewish dietary laws. I could bring you some delicious pork from my father's farm." Rivka would usually just smile at a comment like that.

She, in turn, teased him, "Have you ever eaten *gefilte fish?*" "No, is it good?" he replied. She laughed and promised to save him a piece when her mother next made some.

Conversations about food with religious connotations sometimes led to exchanges about religion. Martin asked, "Has anyone in your larger family ever married a Christian?" Rivka replied, "Not in my family, no, but I've heard that some Jews in town have done this."

One day Beila confronted Rivka about Martin. "Remember," Beila said, "it's all right to talk with men who are not Jewish but you mustn't think about marrying one. Marriage should be with one of your kind. The time will come when you will meet a nice Jewish man that you like, someone like Avram."

Rivka knew that her mother was right, but she often was lonely. Avram had been gone for six years. A girlfriend of hers had become engaged to a fellow from town. He was someone Rivka had rejected as a suitor.

The *shadkhan* tried several times to find a match for Rivka. Each time, her parents encouraged her to give the man a chance, but she would meet with him once, and no more. Each time, she would quietly explain to her mother what it was that she didn't like about the particular suitor—he was too tall, too short, too studious, too serious, too homely. No one pleased her.

She enjoyed spending time with Martin, though she understood that marriage with Martin was out of the question and gradually dismissed from her mind the thought of a future with him.

When Martin saw Rivka out for a stroll, he dropped the reins of the plow or whatever he was doing and trotted to the road to speak with her. He fell into step with her and walked her part of the way home.

On one of these encounters, Martin told Rivka, "This might be our last meeting. My family has arranged for me to stay with cousins in Germany while I am enrolled in a school to study farm management."

Rivka was taken aback. She would miss Martin. She would miss their time together. "I'm sorry you are going, Martin. Maybe after you finish your studies, you'll come back and we can be friends again."

"How good that would be. But my training in Germany will probably last three or four years. Lives can change a lot in that time."

Rivka leaned over and kissed him on the cheek. They parted and waved to each other until both were out of sight.

One of Rivka's few pleasures had disappeared. Wanting to find a new direction for her life, her thoughts increasingly turned to moving away. She thought of moving to town and getting a job there or emigrating to America or South Africa where she had relatives. It would be sad to leave her family, but she could see new places and meet new people.

Soon after her twenty fourth birthday, Rivka became ill. "*Unlucky in love and now unlucky with my health,*" she said to herself. "It's probably just a cold," she told her mother. Then, spots appeared on her arms and legs. A local doctor came to the house and diagnosed it as measles. "It is probably not serious, but it can lead to complications," he remarked. When his examination showed she had a high fever and she reported sharp head-aches, he prescribed medicines and rest and urged her family to isolate her in her room to prevent spreading the disease.

Her fever remained high for a few days. Finally, it broke and the spots on her body began to disappear. Rivka began to eat and get outside a bit. No one else in the family caught the contagious illness. "Why was I chosen for this?" she asked her parents. Neither they nor the doctor could give a good answer. Yetta reminded her of recent solitary walks she had taken. "Maybe you caught it from someone you met,' she surmised.

Gradually, Rivka regained her health and energy. One evening, she suggested to her parents that they emigrate to a place where they would have a more bountiful life. "Listen," said her father, "no matter what, this is our country. Who wants to take chances someplace else?

"We have our farm. Your older brothers and sisters have settled down. Isadore even comes sometimes to help us with the harvest. Things are not great, but they're all right. Soon, Bless the Lord, you will find a husband and life will seem better for you."

"Your father is right," added Beila. "But for you, maybe it's a different story."

Friends who had emigrated wrote her letters about their new lives and encouraged Rivka, in fact her whole family, to follow them. When her mother fell ill, Rivka again reconsidered her plan to leave. With her father working in the fields most of the time, it was incumbent upon her and Yetta to tend to their mother's needs.

Life was increasingly hum drum for Rivka. Each year she tried to arrange for a visit away from home. On one occasion she joined Mariasha and her husband for a week in Vilna. Another time she went with a group of women from the synagogue in Blutz to celebrate an agricultural festival in Shavli. One autumn she traveled all the way to Bialystok to see her friend, Anna Jacobsohn. They had met at the fair in Blutz when they were 18 and wrote to each other frequently. Anna was still single as well.

From the time she entered her thirties, and for eight years thereafter, Rivka grappled with the conflict between her dream to go abroad and her compulsion to care for her mother, who probably could never leave the country because of her illness. One by one, relatives and friends left Lithuania. With each departure, Rivka became more melancholy. She was happy for those leaving but distressed about herself. Rivka wanted to make her own plans.

Then cousin Abe Solomon came for a short visit and talked about going to America. Rivka's life was not likely to change if she stayed in Podblutz. Day after day, week after week, year after year, she carried out the ritual duties of the household and sewed on her machine for small wages. Her life would have few pleasures. Leaving her family behind would be difficult but, after she was settled, she would hope for them to join her.

"Am I destined to spend the rest of my life in this village?" Rivka tearfully asked Yetta on one of their walks. "Will I never have the kind of life Avram and I dreamed about? Can I give up this opportunity? Will I ever have another one like it?" Yetta expressed sympathy. Even though she herself was still a spinster, she was satisfied to stay and care for her mother. If her mother got well, or if she passed away, then she too would go to America.

As the parade of emigrating relatives and friends increased, so did Rivka's dissatisfaction with her sheltered life in the village. A letter from Anna Jacobsohn was the final incentive. Anna had made initial arrangements for travel to America.

Rivka's mind was now set. It was only a matter of confirming her intentions with her family and then making all the necessary preparations for traveling. She had saved enough money from her sewing to meet most of the costs of travel. She knew her family would assist her in ways they could. She arranged to travel with Anna, at least part of the way. Then she would have cousin Abe to accompany her on the longer voyage to America.

Her mind made up, Rivka spoke plainly to her family. "Momma and Poppa, no one loves her family more than I love all of you," she told them with a breaking voice. "Leaving you will be the most difficult thing I'll ever do, but life is passing me by. I have decided to leave, to meet Anna and to join Abe on the ship. I will be the leader for our family in moving to America. I'll work hard so I can send money so that all of you can join me. Please, I ask for your blessings, that you wish me well."

Her father went to Rivka and threw his arms around her. "We have always tried to do the best for you and your sisters and brothers. Your mother and I know how you feel. A few months ago we spoke with Uncle Eliezer. It was his idea to bring Abe here. We want you to go, to be happy. Don't worry about Momma and me; we're getting old. Maybe we will get to America, but maybe not. Distance will only make our love for each other stronger."

Rivka ran to her mother and, with tears in her eyes, kissed her and hugged her. "I love you, Momma." She came back to her father and did the same. Then, she embraced Yetta, saying, "My dear sister, you will have a bigger burden now. I am so grateful to you for all that you've done for Momma and Poppa and me. In America, I will think always about how to bring you, too."

Rivka would join Abe on the same ship to the United States. Abe had proposed marriage, a matter Rivka was uncertain about. She liked him. It excited her that he found her pretty, but she really didn't know him. They would wait until they got to America to decide on a future together.

Her parents encouraged her to see the Rabbi. "The Rabbi is a wise man," said Israel. "It is important that he give you his blessings."

Rivka went. "All these years," said the Rabbi, "I have watched you cope with life's setbacks. You never complained and made your life here. I wish you well on your travels and your new life in America. You are a good and thoughtful person. You stood by your parents for many years. With God's help you will make the right choices."

Rivka could hardly contain her excitement. She sent word to Abe by messenger about approvals from her parents and the Rabbi. Rivka asked him to arrange for ship tickets. It was her idea they would travel separately to Holland, where the ship was located. She would go with Anna as far as Amsterdam. She and Abe would meet in Rotterdam.

Now she had to decide what she would take with her. First, she looked around her room at the things she definitely could not pack. There was the old wooden bed that had been passed down from her grandmother. She had slept in it for the major part of her life. It was dear to her, almost a part of her person. Next to it, on a small table, was the bowl and pitcher she used to wash herself in the mornings and at mealtimes. Although she did not possess a great amount of clothing, she had more than she could possibly take with her. What she left behind could be used by her sisters.

She took down from a shelf a suitcase she had used for the other trips she had taken over the years. It had a hard cover and was worn from usage, but it would suffice to carry most of her items. Rummaging through her clothes cabinet, she picked out three dresses besides the one she would wear while traveling. She spread them in the suitcase, then added under-clothing and stockings and an extra pair of shoes. There was still room for her other personal items and a few pieces of inexpensive jewelry. She then opened a small box where she kept memorabilia and selected a few letters she had saved. She put them in a pocket of the suitcase and then shut it and closed the lock.

She then fetched a large cloth bag with a flower pattern and stuffed a few photographs of her family and some additional letters. That left room for a larger object, one she would want to keep close to her side. Her mother had mentioned giving her a piece of the family's silver items as a remembrance. She hadn't yet learned what that item would be, but she anticipated it was the *menorah* that sat in the entryway. It was not the candelabra the family used for the holidays, but it was a prized possession of her parents.

Rivka finished packing and stopped for a moment to contemplate what might lie ahead. *"America. For years I have been reading about it. Now I will see it for myself."*

CHAPTER 7

▼

The pharmacy on the small side street close to the center of Warsaw had been there for about ten years. Nathan Newman, who had been an apprentice to a pharmacist in Vilna, Lithuania, in the early1880's decided to strike out on his own. He heard that the best opportunities were in Poland, especially in the larger cities. Friends who had moved to Warsaw told him about the need for another pharmacy to serve the Jewish community.

Nathan, his wife Sadie, and their three children had been discussing a prospective move for the past six months. They and their ancestors had strong ties to Vilna. "Just think," said Sadie, "our parents and grandparents lived here and it never entered my mind that we would ever leave this place. Of course, this city is not what it used to be. Jews used to live a happy life here. But now. who could imagine synagogues being destroyed and Jews beaten? I'm asking, Nathan, are things any better for Jews in Warsaw?".

"I cannot believe living conditions in Warsaw can be worse than in Vilna," Nathan remarked to his wife. "My friends there have convinced me it's a good place to start a business. And Jews are not suffering like they are here."

"But Poppa," said their teenage daughter Feyga, "our best friends are still here in Vilna. If we go to Warsaw, we'll never see them again."

"You'll make new friends wherever you go. The important things are for me to earn a good living for my family and for all of us to live a peaceful life. You'll like Warsaw. The Mendels moved there last year and didn't they write they wished they had gone sooner?

"So we're going. I notified the district police and I got the identification papers." The family gathered their belongings and packed as many suitcases as they could find. The Newmans then headed for the train station.

But in Warsaw, like elsewhere in the Pale of Settlement, Jews were segregated. And though Jews made up one third of Warsaw's population, they were crowded into one sixth of the city that made up the Jewish Quarter. Wealthier Jews, those who were the leaders of commerce and banking, lived outside the Pale or at its fringes. Their opulent residences were in stark contrast to the small apartments of the bulk of Warsaw Jews, who daily had to contend with crowded apartments, streets lined with peddlers' pushcarts, and loose garbage and filth in the streets.

"Ooh, those awful smells," said son Julius. "Poppa, Vilna was lots nicer than this place," daughter Sarah added. "Hush, hush, once we get settled into our rooms and you go to school and meet other children, you'll like it here," said Sadie, not quite believing what she was saying.

Nathan managed to rent an apartment close to his friends, who had spoken to a man in charge of a building with a vacancy. A small amount of money secured it for the Newmans. They were lucky. The apartment was a cut above the average residence for Warsaw Jews—away from the center of the Jewish Quarter with larger, sunny rooms.

Nathan and Sadie were satisfied with it. A short walk led to the main Jewish marketplace. Most of the neighbors were Orthodox Jews. A *cheder*, where the children of Orthodox Jews attended school was nearby. The Newman girls went to the girls' *cheder*, even though they were not Orthodox.

Their brother Julius pleaded with his parents to place him in the public school. "Poppa and Momma, I met some boys my age down in the street and they told me what it was like in the boy's *cheder*. They only teach Torah. In Vilna, we learned about other subjects too. I'll still go to synagogue and keep up my Hebrew lessons. Please, I don't want to go to this *cheder*. We're not Orthodox. I'll be unhappy."

"Your mother and I will talk about it. We'll see," said Nathan.

After settling into their apartment, Nathan explored the nearby areas of the city with one of his friends, Osher. They spotted an empty shop on a small street about a mile from where they lived, close to the center of Warsaw.

"It's a good location," said Osher. "It was a clothing store run by an old *goy*. He died recently and his family closed the business. It says here, anyone interested in renting this store should contact the old man's son. He owns the place. The address is here. If you're interested, you can go there."

Nathan squinted as he looked through the glass front and surveyed the space and the remaining store fixtures. "This will be a *good* location for my pharmacy. Jews can get to it easily. Who knows, non Jews might feel comfortable coming here, too. What do you think?"

Osher nodded his head. "You're right. Who could find a better place? And maybe at a bargain price. God willing, you will have a successful business here."

The next morning Nathan found the owner of the shop at his house. He introduced himself. "I just moved here from Vilna and was looking for a place to set up my pharmacy. That empty shop with your name on it seems to be the right kind of place. Maybe even with some of the fixtures. What kind of terms can you offer?"

The owner, a short, blond haired man of about forty, hesitated as he looked Nathan over. "You are a Jew, I suppose."

"Yes, from Vilna."

"Did you have a business in Vilna?"

"Well, not my own. But I worked in a pharmacy there. Now I have enough experience to run my own shop."

"My father devoted his life to his clothing store," said the owner. "I have some good memories of the place. That's now in the past. But I want any business there to have the dignity my father gave to the place."

They discussed details of the rental and came to an agreement on the price. Nathan shook the owner's hand and thanked him.

The owner cautioned him: "You understand, what we agreed to is not final. You have to go to the city government and clear it with them. You'll have to convince the local authorities that this business is justified and you have the proper license. I tell you what. I know people in that office. I think I can help you with it. Maybe you can give *me* a discount on medicine for my family." He laughed. Nathan smiled. "Of course, of course." He then rushed home to tell Sadie of his good fortune.

Nathan knew the success of the business would depend on having a steady clientele. something that didn't come easily unless one had a scheme for making it happen. He knew that his old boss in Lithuania had developed connections with several of the doctors in Vilna and it was the source of most of his sales.

He told Sadie, "I'll start with the Jewish physicians. From there I'll visit other doctors in the area."

Sadie chimed in, "Yeah, that's a good idea. But remember, for every one who agrees to send you customers, you have to put some money in their pocket. That can run up if you make too many deals."

Nathan used part of his savings to stock the store with basic items. With the help of the children, he cleaned and fixed it up. It was a shop to be proud of. Then he set out to see the doctors in the area.

The first Jewish doctor he visited welcomed him to the community. Nathan told about his experience and what his business would be. "You know, I've been referring my patients to the Gentile drugstore near here. There hasn't been a Jewish run pharmacy in this part of Warsaw before. I tell you what. I'll start to refer my Jewish patients to you now. Later on, if they are satisfied, I'll send some of the *goyim* to you as well."

Some of the doctors already had agreements with other pharmacies. All of them, the few Jewish physicians he saw first and the Gentiles ones he visited later, showed respect and took his calling card.

Before long, he had arrangements with several doctors who promised him they would make referrals. When he got home, he told Sadie, "Guess what, only half of them wanted a bribe."

Nathan took great pride in his shop. He tried to model it after the better pharmacies in the city. Customers could see the high quality of products on open shelves. He installed a bench for those with ailments so they could sit while they waited for their medicines to be prepared. If a customer didn't understand what the doctor was recommending, Nathan would explain patiently what the medicine was for.

After ten years, Nathan's Apothecary had become an institution in the community. Nathan's good service, and helpfulness of Nathan and his occasional assistants, brought in more and more people. Sales rose each month, each year. The business was thriving. Income from the drugstore allowed Nathan to move his family to a larger apartment, although it was still in a section of the Jewish Quarter. There were no other Jewish settlements in the city, and it was understood by both government leaders and Jews themselves that Jews would live in the Quarter.

Julius Benjamin Newman was fifteen when the family moved to Warsaw. Since he often spent time after school at his father's pharmacy, he developed a fascination for the store and its contents. He enjoyed gazing at the storefront with the display of the trade in the window—colored jars, packages of bandages, and the symbol of the apothecary profession, a mortar and pestle used in the pharmacist's preparation of some medicines.

Behind the counter were earthen and glass jars of various sizes. All contained medicines or the ingredients needed to produce them—liquids, tablets, ointments, powders, or dry leaves and roots from nature.

Julius was fascinated watching his father mix potions. "What is that for, Papa?" he might say. Or "What makes that mixture turn red?" Nathan would answer each of his questions so that his son could understand and learn.

Julius was proud of his father. He often invited his friends to the shop.

He helped in the store, stocking the shelves and cleaning the floors and the cabinets. As an only son, he escaped military service because the law allowed the oldest male child an exemption from duty.

His father encouraged him to learn the trade. "If you like, I'll teach you about making medicines. Eventually you can take over the business. After all, I'm not getting younger and I won't live forever."

When Julius finished school, Nathan sent him to study with an expert. "I can teach you just so much," Nathan said. "There are professors who can teach you a lot more. I've heard that Janis Hertelis in Riga is one of the best. He is the first Latvian Master in Pharmacy. It'll cost us a bit but, if you are really interested, I'll find the money."

Nathan wasted no time in contacting an acquaintance in Riga who had worked with Hertelis. Within a few weeks, a letter confirming the arrangements was received.

Julius spent four months in Riga. "I couldn't imagine there was that much more to learn about pharmacy," he wrote his father two weeks after he arrived in Riga. "Mr. Hertelis is strict but he is a good teacher."

When he returned to Warsaw, Julius surprised his father with how much he had learned. He had much to tell Nathan about new medicines and procedures. He brought with him the new standards. "Let me give you some examples. If ten pharmacists mix ingredients, the results will not be the same. So now there are official standards so that they are the same.

"Mr. Hertelis also showed us how to best use the ingredients we have. When you put a leaf in a mortar and grind it, something good will result." He picked up a mortar to demonstrate. "But, only part of the leaf has the medicinal benefit. Now we can analyze the contents and separate the important element from the rest." He looked at Nathan with a self satisfying smile.

"That means we can make more effective medicines. I can tell you other things as well."

"Very impressive," Nathan said, returning the smile. "It's amazing what four months of learning can add to your knowledge. I think maybe I have a real partner in my business." He slapped Julius on the back.

Nathan then told his son about a concern of his. "In the best of worlds, a pharmacy like ours can be extremely successful, and I have every reason to think your joining me will make it even more possible. On the other hand, we don't live in the best of worlds." A frown creased his forehead. "Did you notice new markings on the side of our building?"

"No."

"Well they're there and I'm disturbed by it."

A period of relative calm had existed between the Jews and others in Warsaw during the previous year. "We don't know how long it will last," said Nathan. Before they arrived in Warsaw in the early 1880's, there had been many more vicious attacks by peasant groups on Jewish communities. These pogroms had brought damage to Jewish homes and businesses, some deaths, and many injuries to residents in the quarter.

Since the time the Newmans came to Warsaw, there had been fewer attacks. Still, foul rumors were spread among the peasants, like one that said Jews were killing Gentile children and using their blood in preparation of holiday matzohs. Such rumors without base spread from time to time. When the economy slumped, Jews were held responsible for the decline and punished.

Nathan's Apothecary was targeted several times. On a few occasions the storefront window was broken and the building defaced. "Jews were Christ killers." "Wealthy Jews deprive peasants of their livelihood." Sometimes, a caricature of a long nosed Jew and a Star of David were drawn on a building to "mark" the presence of Jews.

Nathan and his family were shaken by these events, but they were intent on staying and continued to make a good living in the city. Besides, conditions were no better in Vilna. Most Jews were frightened by the attacks but they tried to overlook them and convince themselves that they could survive them without much harm.

"These attacks come in spells." said Nathan to his son. "So long as no one here is hurt, we can manage. The City Council is beginning to pay attention, especially to the Jew on the Council. Maybe soon we'll get some protection."

Some of Nathan's and Sadie's families had emigrated to America. Nathan's relatives had written:

"You don't find such violent treatment of Jews here in the New World. Life in the United States may not be all that we expected, but at least it is safe."

Others they knew had gone to South Africa, England, and even Australia. All of them encouraged the Newmans to follow suit. In each place, they found personal freedoms that were forbidden to Jews in most parts of Eastern Europe.

Nathan, nervous about the rising attacks, thought about America. "Maybe I can reestablish my business there. If not, I could find work as a pharmacist," he told Sadie. "Our savings will help our family to live comfortably."

Sadie and their daughters, Sarah and Feyga, had long talks about leaving Poland, about going to a place where Jews were not treated harshly. There wasn't a complete meeting of minds. "I don't know," said Sadie. "My head tells me we should leave, but my heart speaks of our ancestors who stayed and suffered here in Europe."

Feyga had read about America. "Momma," she said, "I know how you feel but I hope to have a long life still ahead of me, and I would like to be somewhere where I can enjoy it."

Sarah turned to her parents, "For a long time I wasn't afraid. But now things are changing, for the worst. My friend Ruth's cousin was killed during a riot in Lodz. Are we going to stay here until one of us is killed? Let's get out of here now." She was usually not an emotional person, but the tense situation had made her more fearful.

Julius did not feel the same way as the rest of his family about leaving Poland. "Look, we've built up a good business here and now I'm making a contribution. Is this a time to leave?

"I don't want to leave now. I'm not saying the rest of you shouldn't go, but I want to remain here. Poppa, turn over the pharmacy to me. I know I can keep the business going. Whatever profits I get from it will be yours, after I take out what I need to live here."

Sadie, her face showing concern, said, "I think you're making a mistake, Julius, but if that's what you want, so be it. Remember, you can always change your mind."

Julius's parents and sisters completed preparations to leave for America. A cousin had even arranged a job for Nathan. a good position in a large pharmacy.

Julius accompanied them as they made their way to the railroad station.

"It pains me to have us separate," Julius told his family, "but I know I'm making the right decision. I'm grateful to you, Poppa, for giving me a chance to keep the pharmacy here. I'll pay you back for your investment as soon as I can accumulate enough cash." He embraced his father. Nathan wiped his eyes with a handkerchief.

Julius went over to his mother and hugged her for a long time. Tears came to Mrs. Newman's eyes and she stroked her son's hair. "I think you're doing the wrong thing, but what do I know? I'm only your mother."

He then moved to his sisters. "Sarah and Feyga, thank you for being so understanding. I couldn't have more loving sisters." They clung to him.

"I'll write to you regularly. Who knows? I may visit you in America before too long." He embraced them all again and got embraced in return. As he left the station, he turned around several times to wave to them as they pressed their faces on the train windows.

Although he had several Jewish friends, Julius also developed friendships with local Catholic boys from his earlier school days.

When Julius wasn't working in the pharmacy, he and his Catholic friends played football together. They roamed several areas of the city—the parks, the business district, streets with shops—and, like most young men, ogled pretty girls.

Religion would not often be a topic of conversation, except when one of his Catholic friends would make an offhand negative remark about Jews. It was a reflex reaction for most of them. Sometimes they caught themselves and told Julius, "We don't mean you." He learned to put up with such remarks and felt he had some positive influence on their feelings about Jews. His friends respected Julius and were impressed by his intellect and ambition.

One friend, Francis, once remarked, "You've got a good brain, Julius. Have you thought about going to the university?" It pleased Julius to hear friends speak of him that way. His typical reply was "I'm happy with being a pharmacist, and I couldn't afford to go to the university anyway."

Julius's study in Latvia gave him a reputation as a medical expert among those who knew him. He served as a "substitute doctor" for his friends when they were injured or complained about not feeling well.

His friends attended daily Mass at St. Casimir, a distinctive structure with a large green dome over a white façade. Sometimes they invited him to join them, but he always begged off and said he had to go to the pharmacy. He knew his parents would not be pleased and he would feel uncomfortable himself. Even though he wasn't an especially observant Jew, it had never occurred to him to explore the possibility of examining other religions.

Then one day, feeling somewhat isolated in his group, he thought to himself, "*Why not? It might be interesting to see what takes place.*" He surprised them one Sunday by inviting himself.

The experience was eye opening. Compared to the Spartan synagogue, the church was large and ornate. Julius found the stained glass windows stunning. The priest's vestments were elaborate. His brightly colored chasuble and linen tunic covered with lace particularly caught Julius's eye. The statues and incense were mesmerizing. Above all, there was the opportunity to atone for sins every day. He considered that Jews had a single Day of Atonement each year. His friends told him the confession box allowed a confidential audience with one of the priests.

Julius was entranced, although he did not let his feelings be known to his friends until sometime later. Every once in a while he went to mass with them. "Just an observer," he remarked. His friends were pleased.

Although Julius appeared confident about his decision to remain in Warsaw, he was already thinking about his future in Poland. Maintaining his father's pharmacy would provide an adequate income. Instead of staying in the family residence in the Jewish Quarter, which had more space than he needed and was too expensive to maintain, he worked out an arrangement with one of his friends, Joseph, to share a small apartment away from the ghetto.

Julius received a letter from his father:

My dear Julius,

I hope the business is going well and you are adjusting to life in Warsaw without us.

It took us a while to get settled in New York, but everything is good at the moment. Where I work is a large pharmacy with several pharmacists. At first, I thought I couldn't adjust to not being my own boss but it's all right. In fact, it's nice to have people to talk with who know what you're doing, and what I get paid plus what Sarah makes takes care of our needs very well.

Our apartment is no better than what we had in Warsaw, but we enjoy New York very much. We can go where we please and there is a great deal we can do and see.

Your mother misses you a lot, as we all do. Stay well. Your father

Julius replied:

Dear Family,

I was happy to get Poppa's letter and find out you are all doing well.

The business is fine. I still have many customers from the old neighborhood and some from the other sections of the city. A young fellow is helping me in the shop. He doesn't know much about pharmacy but he is a hard worker and is polite with customers. It gives me a chance to take off a little time every once in a while.

The big news is that I moved out of our apartment and am now sharing a small place with my friend, Joseph. I don't remember if you had met him. I got to know him through another friend, Francis. I think you did meet him. He's tall and thin and has dark hair. His father used to come to our shop. It felt a little strange living with someone not in my family, but I think it's a good idea. It is much less expensive, and the money I save can be put back into the business.

That's all for now. Keep sending me letters. Love, Julius

Once his family was gone, he stopped attending synagogue, which he had been doing at least sporadically before they left. He believed dropping his Jewish connections meant he would have greater freedom to participate in the city's activities and broaden his citywide contacts. Being 'one of them' would recast his world and make him a real citizen of Warsaw. The Jews he had as customers would still come to his shop since they lacked good alternatives.

His friend, Joseph, was a happy go lucky type, prone to cracking jokes and playing tricks on unsuspecting victims. Julius enjoyed his company and listened to his tales about happenings in the factory where he worked. The environment was in stark contrast to that of Julius' previous home life, where formality and protocol prevailed. If there was a serious side to Joseph, it was in his devotion to the Church. He often brought up the topic in discussions with Julius.

When Julius was urged by his friends to join the Church, it did not seem like such a far fetched idea. After first struggling with the notion, he agreed to it. He was becoming more fascinated with Catholicism and convinced himself it was the right thing to do.

To disguise his Jewish given names, Julius Benjamin became known as James (at least, among non Jews). He kept his surname, which was that of a famous Cardinal who had converted from the Church of England. Julius regretted ending visits to his friends in the Jewish ghetto.

Julius went to St. Casimir's and was assigned to Brother Thomas, a young priest close to his own age. He explained how his Catholic friends and chance attendance had led him to want to become a Catholic. Brother Thomas told him the steps he needed to take.

At the conclusion of his meetings with Thomas, Julius secluded himself in his room and contemplated what he had been undertaking. Catholicism was strange to him but it had a fundamental appeal in that it helped him share religious thoughts with his Catholic friends.

His conscience bothered him a little, so he sent off a letter to his younger sister:

Dearest Sarah,

I know you've seen my letters to the family. This one I am sending to you because I have a matter to discuss that may trouble Momma and Poppa.

You now know I left the Jewish Quarter and am living with a fellow named Joseph. The point is that he's Catholic. You know I've always had Catholic as well as Jewish friends in Warsaw. Joseph and Francis are now my two best friends and they believe strongly in Catholicism. That didn't bother me for a while, but recently they asked me to come to Church with them. I refused them several times and then, one day, I felt what harm would it be to join them once.

What I have to say is that I've now become interested in the Church and am going more often. I even spoke with some of the priests there and am considering conversion. Does that bother you?

I will leave it up to you whether or not you tell Momma and Poppa. We were never highly religious Jews but Jews nevertheless. Maybe it's too early to say anything to them. I could end up changing my mind.

How do you like your job? Does New York suit your tastes?

Your loving brother Julius

He soon got a letter back from Sarah:

Dear Julius,

Your last letter came as something of a shock. I am not one to preach. Yet, you should really think things through before you make such a critical decision in your life. I know you must be lonely and it is a comfort to have people to be with. That doesn't mean you have to change your religion to do so. What is curious is that for centuries Jews had no choice but to convert to Christianity or be slaughtered. You have other choices you can make. Look at the possibilities first.

No, I have not said anything about it to Momma and Poppa. If you continue with Catholicism I will have to tell them. Please keep me informed about your decision.

I like my job in the Manhattan Needleworks Company. It's hard work spending hour upon hour at a sewing machine, but it's a good company and the money I get helps out at home.

We love you and are concerned for you. I look for the day you realize that New York is where you belong and you come to join us. Lovingly, Sarah

A few months later, he wrote to Sarah to tell her he was taking the big step but not to assume he is a different person. Religion is only one part of life, he told her.

No matter how hard he tried, aspects of the religion still troubled him. Most importantly, he hadn't grasped the concept of the Trinity. "Maybe further study will help me to accept it," he mused. He did find appealing the group participation in church, something he found lacking in Jewish services. He convinced himself he was on the right track from a spiritual perspective.

There were, of course, many practical aspects to his conversion. He felt welcomed to the fold. He was warmly greeted when he went to the church. Many of the parishioners stopped to talk with him, if only to exchange pleasantries. And even though Warsaw was within the Pale of Settlement, the Russians would not likely try to do harm him as a Catholic. While the Russian Orthodox Church did not look too kindly on Catholics, they saved their utmost hatred for Jews.

Julius believed he would become more accepted in the community and his business would even prosper as a result. Catholics were inclined to purchase their pharmaceuticals where they knew the proprietors. Although Jews made up a substantial proportion of his customers, the addition of more Catholics would expand his clientele.

One day in their apartment, Julius and Joseph get into a heated discussion about his attendance at church. "You are not going to Mass as often as you should," said Joseph. Julius countered: "Why is it so important to attend regularly if you maintain your beliefs and pray daily?" "I can see you haven't learned your lessons well," replied Joseph. There was no meeting of minds on this topic.

From time to time people from the old neighborhood reminded him of his Jewish background when they came to the pharmacy. One old Jewish man commented caustically: "We don't see you in synagogue any more, not even in the neighborhood. Have you turned on your religion? Your parents would not be pleased." And more often than he wished, among Catholic friends his ears picked up anti Semitic remarks, not necessarily aimed at him but disturbing nevertheless.

Time progressed and his Catholic training was advancing. For him it was like going to school. He was learning something new almost every day. It tickled his intellectual curiosity as well as prepared him for what he regarded as his "new religion."

Despite what Joseph said and Brother Thomas's instruction, Julius could not accept every tenet of the church. After all, even his Catholic friends didn't observe every ritual. As a Jew, he was not committed to all aspects of what he was taught, and it should be the same now. So long as he conformed in essence, that should be enough.

Increasingly, Julius tried to come to grips with who he really was and what he wanted out of life. Being a pharmacist satisfied him, as did the feeling that he was contributing to the health of the community. He was gratified that many people relied on him for expert knowledge.

As for his personal life, there was much to be desired. He had no regular girlfriend. He met young women at dances and parties but had formed no lasting relationships. Julius missed his family.

He began to seek consolation in frequent trips to the red light district of the city. He engaged several prostitutes to satisfy his sexual urges, but he was repelled by their appearance and impersonal behavior.

On one occasion, he was sent to meet a somewhat older woman. She seemed familiar. She, too, recognized him. "Aren't you Feyga's brother?

Hesitatingly, he replied, "Yes, you know her?"

"We were in school together."

"You mean *cheder*?

"That's right. Even Jewish women have to make a living."

Julius was shaken. He left quickly. All the way home, he kept thinking that this could have been Feyga or Sarah, if the circumstances were different. His visits to the red light district ceased.

The more he assessed his religious situation, the more doubts arose in his mind about the direction he was going. He realized he'd been fooling himself about being a Catholic. He was hungry for new relationships. There was a void he was trying to fill when his family went to America. True, he wasn't a good Jew but that was the religion of his upbringing. It wasn't just a religious matter. It was a cultural one, too. He just couldn't forget the traditions, the holidays. They still had some meaning to him. He had learned a lot about Catholicism and could see good points about the religion, but it was not for him.

He showed up one night at a social meeting of young men and women in the Jewish Quarter. It was a weekly event that he attended a few times when his family was in Warsaw. The young people would gather to play music and talk about common problems over coffee. It was also a good place for men and women to meet and romance.

It was the first time Julius had gone there in a long while. He sheepishly stayed at the back of the room, unsure about how he would be received.

Several people recognized him and came over. "Good to see you here, Julius. We've missed you. Come join our table. How's the business? We heard you were converting to Catholicism. Is that true?"

He was introduced to a woman he had not met before.

"I didn't hear. What is your name?" asked Julius.

"Etta."

"That's a sweet name. I haven't seen you before. Have you lived in Warsaw long?"

"About a year. My family moved here from Riga. I haven't seen you here before. Are you new to Warsaw?"

"No, no, my family came here about ten years ago, from Vilna. My parents and sisters went to New York over a year ago. I have a pharmacy not too far from here. I haven't been to the social evening for some time, though. I'm glad I came tonight."

"Actually, this is my last time at this gathering. Next week I am heading for America, too. My brother is already there.

"How does your family like New York?" she added.

His parents and sisters had indeed been writing to him about their life in New York. Much of it sounded very exciting.

"My family writes that they live in a Jewish area of the city but not in a restricted area like in Warsaw. My father says he's as happy being a pharmacist working for someone else as he was running his own shop. My sisters tell me they are enjoying the New World even more than they had expected. So, maybe I have to see for myself."

His father had written recently:

"I read in the newspaper here that Jews in Poland were being treated badly. Is that true in our old neighborhood? And what about our shop? Has it gotten even worse than before we left, or is it more of the same thing?"

A police officer came to the pharmacy one day for what seemed at first like a routine business check. Julius remembered such a visit a year earlier, but he didn't recall what he was asked then. Something about his business license. He never heard anything more about it.

This time, after asking to see his business license, the officer copied down some of the information. Then he inquired about Julius's parents. He asked questions that were written in a notebook. "Where are they now? Did they have passports? Did they plan on returning to Poland? How much money did they take with them?"

Julius answered as best he could. He asked why he was being questioned about his parents. The policeman replied in a gruff voice, "We're just updating our records." The questions made Julius feel uncomfortable. He wanted to tell the officer to leave but thought better of it. After fifteen minutes or so, the officer left without the courtesy of a goodbye.

Julius wondered if the police were checking on Jews. Or perhaps whether the government was going to start taxing people for the assets their families took with them.

He began visiting the old neighborhood more often, and spending time with his old friends. He was greeted by several former friends. Some commented to him, "Still a *goy*?" or "Maybe you now see the light." It seems that people in the old neighborhood found him a juicy topic of conversation.

On one of his walks in the Quarter, he spotted the old man who had earlier berated him at his store. They nodded to each other. He had stopped seeing his Catholic friends and had moved out of Joseph's apartment. He was back renting a room in the Jewish Quarter.

Though Julius was glad to have returned to the Quarter, he was also disturbed about frequent reports of police actions against Jews in the city. A headline in the newspaper one day read:

STRIKES BY SOCIAL DEMOCRAT WORKERS IN WARSAW AND OTHER POLISH CITIES. JEWS CHARGED AS INSTIGATORS

Anti Semitic riots were taking place around the country with increased frequency. Often they were led by peasant groups, with Czarist militia not far behind. Jews spent less time in the streets and more time in their apartments to avoid personal contacts with non Jews.

He wrote to his father and related what had happened.

> "Yes, what is happening to Jews in Warsaw might not be different than before but it is making me uneasy. I am seriously thinking about joining you in New York."

Without much fanfare, Julius put the pharmacy up for sale. He agonized over it. His father had devoted so much of his time and effort to build up the business and Julius had worked hard to keep it prosperous.

Customers were drifting away. The building had become a convenient target for rioters.

Julius sold the business to a Christian pharmacist from the other side of the city for a sum far lower than what Julius knew it was worth. After paying taxes and fees to the city government, he had enough left to get a passport and to book passage on the S. S. Netherlands. He would travel to Boulogne, France, to get on the ship which would take him to New York.

Julius regretted he would not be able to pay his father back as he had once said he would.

He wrote to his sister and told her his plans.

"With some luck, I will be meeting all of you in New York.

CHAPTER 8

▼

Early in 1893, Abe Solomon, Rivka Borchowitz, and Julius Newman had each booked passage on the S.S. Netherlands for its May departure for America. Each would follow a different path from their home to the ship.

The documents Abe obtained for himself and Rivka were valid and secure. Some travelers were turned away when their documents were found to be fakes. He followed the advice of some friends who recommended traveling with as little luggage as possible.

"A light load is easier to transport. It will also mean not as much inspection by authorities," he was told. He took only one large bag containing only what he considered essential, plus a few sentimental items like letters and photographs.

As to his house, Abe didn't know what to do with all the furniture and household goods, his sewing machine, and all the items his family had left behind. He worked it out with Uncle Eliezer to maintain it for a while, so the authorities wouldn't suspect that he didn't intend to return. Later, Eliezer would be able to sell the house and contents and maybe send the money to Abe in America.

As he walked through the village, he informed his friends and neighbors that he was leaving. "What will the *shtetl* be without you?" they said. "May your future life hold great joy!" said another. The Rabbi gave a blessing for his safe travel.

One of Abe's neighbors took him by cart to the railway station in the provincial capital of Kovno to get a train to Berlin. Before they left Kraglova, Abe asked the neighbor to take him to the small Jewish graveyard. There Abe went to the burial site of his dear wife, Bessie, and with tears in his eyes he recited a prayer for the dead. He then lifted himself back onto the cart and motioned for the neighbor to continue to the station.

"Thank you, thank you, good friend," Abe bid his neighbor, and they said their goodbyes. "I'll send you a letter from America." Abe grabbed his belongings and climbed the steps to the main station level. Only a few people were on the platform, as it was still early for the train arrival. He made his way to the ticket agent's booth to assure himself his tickets were in proper order. There was one person ahead of him. In a few minutes, he moved up to the window.

"I am going to Berlin," Abe said nonchalantly. "Do I have the right ticket here?" The agent looked up at him suspiciously and then lowered his gaze to inspect the ticket.

"Where is your passport?" He stared coldly at Abe until the passport was produced. "What is the purpose of your trip?"

Abe told him he was going to visit friends in Berlin. "We haven't seen each other for a long time," he said, trying to act casual.

"But you only have a one way ticket. Where is your return ticket?" the agent asked in a challenging way.

Abe had anticipated this question. "I don't have one yet. I wasn't sure how long I would stay with my friends. I thought it would be best if I got my return ticket in Berlin when I was certain when I would come back. It could be maybe two weeks, maybe three weeks."

The agent resumed his skeptical look, turned the pages of the passport several times, and locked Abe's eyes with a steely glare. "Well, all right," he said, "but don't delay getting your return ticket. You should know the trains can be crowded this time of year. Don't count on being able to come back exactly when you want to."

Abe thanked him, stuffed the ticket and passport into his jacket pocket, grabbed his bag, and headed out to the railway platform. It was a sunny mid morning. In the meantime, with a half hour to wait for the train, Abe walked to the far end of the platform and sat on a bench. He pulled out a small book he had started reading at home. He did not want to engage in conversation.

When the train pulled into the station, Abe found one of the second class cars and stepped up into it. He went to the far end for a single seat. No one could be seated right next to him. Several people followed and took seats in the car.

A whiff of smoke drifted past his nostril. He disliked smoking, but there was no place on the train where he could escape it.

The train was old and shabby. The seats were dirty, the armrests smudged and sticky. Some of the seats in his car were missing bolts that fastened them to the floor.

He lifted his bag onto a rack above the seat and made himself as comfortable as he could. He peered out the window to see the conductor signaling the closing of doors. The train pulled out of the station. Having stayed up late the previous night, Abe was in need of sleep, so he leaned back and began to doze off.

Soon the train conductor entered the car and woke him. "Your ticket and passport, please."

Abe gave a jerk. He opened his eyes, sat upright, and slowly took the documents out of the pocket inside his jacket. The conductor glanced at Abe a couple of times but said nothing. He punched the ticket and returned the documents and moved on to other passengers.

Abe tried to stay awake but he kept nodding off. Each time someone brushed by him or he heard an unusual sound like a window frame rattling, he awakened with a start. At one point, the conductor passed through the car and announced softly, "Dinner is now being served in the dining car." Abe opened his eyes and stretched. He looked around, but no one in his car was heading for the diner.

He stood up, reached into his bag, and pulled out a small package containing some brown bread and hard cheese. He also pulled out a small jug holding a beverage.

When he started eating, he thought about the Kraglova he left behind. He considered going back some day, but the political situation would have to change a lot before he would do that.

Abe mumbled to himself, "All of these decisions about leaving and traveling have put my head in a spin! To make matters worse, I will have plenty more decisions to make before I get to America."

The train stopped every few hours to pick up passengers at Polish cities and to load water for the steam engine. Each time, Abe peered out the window to observe who was entering and leaving his car. Once he was satisfied that nothing unusual was happening, he shut his eyes.

Whenever he awakened, he read from his book or did some stitching on a suit he was sewing for himself. When the train stopped to add coal or water, he climbed down the steps at the end of the car to inhale the fresh air.

At one such stop, a small girl approached him and tried to sell him some flowers.

"How much do you want for them?" he asked.

"One ruble."

Abe had little cash, but he felt sorry for the girl. She was shabbily dressed and extremely thin. He pulled out a ruble, gave it to her, and took the flowers. "Thank you," she said, curtsying, and smiling. He smiled back. He looked at the flowers. Maybe, he thought, there was some way he could keep them alive until he met Rivka. He returned to his seat and placed the flowers carefully on top of his luggage.

Perhaps ten hours into the trip the train lurched and came to a stop. Abe jumped up and looked out the window. They had reached the German border. Two officials, one German and one Polish, boarded the train and made their way through the cars.

When they got to Abe, they asked for his passport and quizzed him about where he was going and why. Most of the questions came from the Polish agent. Abe repeated the story he told the station agent in Kovno. The official asked for the address in Berlin where he can be reached. Abe hesitated briefly and then gave an address of someone he knew a long time ago. It was unlikely that person was still living there, but it was also unlikely the authorities would check it out.

The two agents moved to the other end of the car and had a short conversation, looking back at Abe a few times. Finally, they made their way into the next car. Abe thought, "If they check that Berlin address, I'm in trouble."

It was after midnight when the train arrived in Berlin. The first part of his trip had now been completed. Abe now waited for the train that would take him to Amsterdam. The railway station was largely vacated at that hour. A few policemen were making their rounds. Abe had to ask for directions to the track for the Amsterdam train, but he made sure his questions were directed to people who looked Jewish or to German peasants who probably would not care who he was.

Abe kept his tickets buttoned inside a pocket he had sewn into his jacket. He removed them for the first time. Abe continued to be cautious about who he spoke with and how he behaved.

Daylight appeared before the train reached Amsterdam. Abe could see the countryside in Holland, the well kept fields, windmills, animals, and people on their way to work, some walking and others on bicycles. It was a pleasant sight.

The train pulled into the depot at Amsterdam. The mood was serene. There were no policemen on the platforms. Everyone seemed to be going about their business calmly and purposefully.

Abe was directed by a railway agent to an adjoining station where he could get the Rotterdam train. "Just go out that exit on the right and cross the street," the agent said. "You'll come directly to the tracks where your train will be." Abe thanked him and walked toward the exit.

It was just a short distance to Rotterdam. For the first time since he left home he was greeted with smiling people. It was reassuring.

He had timed the journey so he would arrive in Rotterdam a couple of days before the final departure date. A friend directed him to a hotel where Jewish travelers were welcome. By design, Rivka would meet him there.

He located the hotel and took a room. Exhausted from his long journey, he removed his clothing, wrapped himself with a towel, peeked outside the door to make sure no one was passing by, and wandered down the hall to the common bath area.

Rivka Borchowitz arrived at Rotterdam by a different route. Her friend Anna Jacobsohn's trans Atlantic ship was to leave Amsterdam the same day Rivka's ship departed Rotterdam. The two would travel to Amsterdam together. Rivka had only to make the short trek to Rotterdam by herself.

Rivka and Anna met in Joniskis, Lithuania. Rivka arrived by cart and Anna by train.

"It's so wonderful to see you again," said Rivka. "I can't believe it's been a year since we last saw each other at the fair in Blutz?"

"Yes, it seems like ages. How are your parents? When you last wrote, you were worried about your mother."

"My mother's health is not good and she worries about me traveling such a long distance, but she is holding up well and my father is fine. It was difficult leaving them. I pray that they can join me before too long. What about your parents?"

"I hope we will see them in America before too long."

From Joniskis the women took a train that went directly to Libau, the major Latvian take off point for emigrants to the New World. As they made their way to the right track, the women had to listen to vulgarities from men they passed. "Don't even look at them," whispered Anna, and they moved as quickly as they could. "What language," said Rivka. "We don't even talk to our animals that way."

One of the men seemed to be following them toward the track, which unnerved Rivka. His remarks shocked them, but they acted as if they didn't hear. "How crude some men can be," whispered Anna. "They are low life," responded Rivka. "I hope we don't find that type on the ship."

Rivka told Anna, "I'm glad we're together. I'd be frightened if I were alone." On the train, the women relaxed a bit.

Once in Libau, they spent a night at the home of an acquaintance of Anna's. The following morning the women set sail on a small freighter for Amsterdam. The freighter was filled with agricultural products bound for Scandinavia. It had space for about fifteen passengers.

Anna and Rivka shared a small room. Since it was not a passenger ship, it was not outfitted for travel comfort. Nevertheless, the room and facilities were adequate. The women knew they were better off than they would be in steerage on a passenger ship. Two thick pallets were next to each other on the floor and there was a small cabinet in which to put their belongings. A small wooden chair and metal table took up the rest of the space. There was a toilet at the end of the hallway, which they shared with others in the same corridor.

At mealtimes, the travelers joined the freighter's employees in a dining room. Some of the passengers were only going as far as Stockholm or Copenhagen, others to Amsterdam. A few besides Anna and Rivka were linking with ships heading for America. The crew outnumbered the passengers by two to one. The Captain held forth in the dining room and maintained decorum.

The food was simple but plentiful, with large portions meant for the working crew. Anna and Rivka knew they could not keep the kosher tradition and ate what was served to them.

The Captain, who spoke several languages, engaged in conversation with all of the travelers. He dealt strictly with his crew but was cordial with passengers. Anna and Rivka found him fascinating because he liked to tell interesting tales of his earlier voyages. The women talked with a few of the other passengers who could converse in Lithuanian or German. They mostly shared information about themselves and their future plans. The crew had been instructed not to talk to the travelers unless asked for a service. They proved to be well behaved on the trip, for which Anna and Rivka were grateful.

Throughout the trip, passengers were allowed freedom to roam around the freighter except into the operational areas. The opportunity to get out of their small room and roam around the deck was gratifying for the women.

Rivka and Anna proved to be good traveling companions. They spent many hours on deck inhaling the fresh northern air. They exchanged stories and speculated on what America will be like.

"I heard that in New York Harbor there is a statue of a woman so tall you can barely see the top," said Rivka.

"That's what they call the Statue of Liberty. It's supposed to be welcoming people like us to America."

"I can hardly wait to see it."

"Which cousin did you say was meeting you when you arrive?"

"Sheyna Goetz. She's my cousin and Abe's too, so she'll be waiting for both of us."

"Since you and I will both be in the New York area, we should be able to visit with each other."

These conversations made the time pass by more quickly than if they were traveling alone.

Both women had left most of their belongings behind. Anna carried two medium sized valises. Rivka had a large suitcase and a bulging canvas bag.

During the trip, Anna asked Rivka, "Why do you keep that bag so close to you all the time?"

"It has some personal things that are important." She opened the bag part way to reveal a package of letters her sisters and brothers had written to her wishing her well on her travels. She also pulled out photographs of her family they had given her if she got homesick. Then, stretching open the bag as far as she could, she showed Anna a silver menorah. It wasn't large, but it had places for seven candles.

Anna ran her fingers over the shining candelabra and smiled. "It's beautiful."

"This menorah is precious," said Rivka. "Not only because it is made of silver, but because it was my grandmother's. Maybe even my great grand-mother's, I don't know. My mother insisted I take it. She said it will always remind me of my family." Her eyes moistened a bit. "Wherever I live in America, it will occupy a special place."

They talked about what each had read recently. Anna had a better education than Rivka, having gone to secondary school; yet, both had good minds and enjoyed reading and discussing books.

Anna told about her family. Her father was a leather worker and her mother worked as a clerk at a manufacturing company. Her brother was learning their father's trade. "Together they make a decent income," she said. "As for me, I work in a library. Not much money, but I have all those books to read and I can take them home."

Anna revealed she had a boyfriend who had recently gone to America. "It's the only time I've ever really been in love. My heart longs for him so much. I don't know if I can contain myself until I meet him in New York," she said with great emotion.

"We knew each other in school a number of years ago. Then we lost touch until last year. He's now a writer and wants to work at a newspaper. Someone gave him a letter of introduction to a newspaper in New York. He was so excited.

"We met again by chance in Bialystok and fell in love. Like you and Abe, we decided to wait to marry until we get to America. He's already there. Can you see now why I'm in a hurry to get to New York?"

Rivka hugged Anna. "Can you believe it? Two old maids on the way to meet their future husbands." They giggled together. They were now both very relaxed and prepared to enjoy the rest of the trip with great joy.

As the freighter proceeded through the Baltic Sea, the temperatures dropped rapidly and the women wrapped themselves with blankets when they got out of their cabin. The vistas were spectacular. Approaching Stockholm, they could see the lush lowlands of Sweden and, in the distance, the mountains of both Sweden and Norway.

After a brief stop to leave off passengers and freight in Stockholm, the freighter worked its way through a twisted network of waterways toward Copenhagen. Again, after unloading its cargo, it headed out for the open area of the North Sea and toward Amsterdam.

In Amsterdam, the crew bid farewell to the women. Anna was a more experienced traveler and accompanied Rivka to the train station. The two women embraced. "Remember," said Anna, "Promise me you will meet me in New York the first opportunity you get. Here is the address where I'll be staying, at least for the first few weeks." She scribbled the address on a piece of paper.

"I promise, I promise," Rivka pledged.

Anna cautioned Rivka about accepting help from men on the way to Rotterdam. "You can never be too careful," she admonished her. "When you get to Rotterdam, go immediately to meet Abe." She turned and headed out of the station, glancing back and waving to Rivka several times.

Rivka found the Rotterdam train fairly easily. The trip took less than an hour, and she felt very comfortable in the presence of other riders. At Rotterdam, she asked a train agent for directions to the hotel. It turned out to be only a short walk from the station. Along the way, she stopped from time to time to glance into shop windows.

Rivka found the Jewish transient hotel and reunited with Abe as planned. It was a joyous event for both of them. They embraced, each showing the emotion that had built in both in the months since they had last seen each other.

"Abe, I'm so happy to see you. I was afraid I might not find you here. What can I say? I really missed you."

Abe's smile was from ear to ear. "The two days of waiting had seemed like two months. You are even more beautiful than when I last saw you." She blushed. Abe handed her the flowers he'd bought from the girl. "They lost some color, but they're still flowers." The two hugged and kissed each other again.

Hand in hand, they wandered to a small grassy area beyond the hotel and found a bench to sit on.

"I keep looking at my ticket and making sure what I need is in my bag," said Abe. "I think about taking the ship across the ocean and getting to New York. I try to forget what I left in Kraglova. But it is not easy. My stomach is turning and I get a headache from worrying about everything."

"You would not be human if you didn't have those feelings. For me, it's the same. I left my family behind. I'm going to a place I know very little about. Whether or not I can get a good job remains a question. Why shouldn't we be nervous?"

"Of course, we are not alone," added Abe. "There are others going now and many, including our cousins, who have gone before us."

"That's true," Rivka replied. "We are part of a chain of people who hope to keep Judaism alive. Our families go back in time, even to those mentioned in the Bible. It wasn't strange for many of them to move to a new location, especially when they were threatened. We are doing our part."

"You are such a sensible person, Rivka, and you are so easy to love."

They smiled at each other and hugged once again.

Julius Newman traveled to Boulogne to embark on the S. S. Netherlands.

In order to keep a low profile about his decision to leave Poland and join his family, he arranged for a passport and ship ticket through non governmental local agents without telling his friends or former neighbors or the Church. He wanted to leave without calling special attention to himself.

Before leaving Warsaw, Julius stopped shaving. It gave his youthful face a more mature look. His black beard grew slowly, but by the time he was on the ship, it would be quite full.

Julius had learned about clandestine means of travel out of the country through one of the customers in his pharmacy. He belonged to a network of people, both Jews and non Jews, who found safe passage for Jews trying to slip out of Warsaw and assisted them to their destinations. Of course, it required payments of money to a few people. His customer arranged for Julius to meet a man in Warsaw who made the arrangements.

Julius was spirited first to the country house of a Catholic farmer outside the city where a middle aged Jewish couple was also waiting for transportation westward. A peasant with a horse and cart put Julius and his two companions in the cart, carefully spreading a cloth over them. He took them twenty kilometers down the road to the border with Czechoslovakia.

About half way to their destination, the peasant saw militiamen on horseback. He reined in his horse, called back to the three to remain quiet, jumped off the cart, and trotted into a wooded area to relieve himself. The soldiers slowed down and looked in his direction. He shouted to them, "Everything is all right. I couldn't wait until I got to where I was going.

The potatoes in the cart make a heavy load. I can't go very fast." The soldiers laughed, gestured to him in a vulgar way, and moved on.

The peasant stopped at the border to be cleared through the Polish gate, which required the presentation of passports and work papers. The peasant and the Jewish couple showed theirs, were asked a few questions, and were allowed through.

Julius met some resistance. The guards looked over his papers and told him to come down from the cart. They told the peasant to pull over to the side of the road. "What is the problem?" Julius asked. "Everything should be in order."

A police officer studied Julius's documents and looked at him. "Your passport says you are Catholic. But your work papers show you are a Jew. Which is it?"

The question caught Julius off guard. He struck a confident pose. "Let me explain. I am now Catholic. I belong to the Church in Warsaw. I am not a Jew anymore." The policemen talked among themselves for an extended period and then returned to him. One of them asked, "Where are you going?"

"I am headed for France. I have business there."

The guards conferred again, returned his papers, and told him to go ahead now but to fix his papers when he went home.

His driver and the couple waited for Julius. They became frightened by the experience, not knowing what would happen to Julius, or to them for that matter. Julius climbed back into the cart and sat down with little show of emotion.

After next being cleared by the Czech sentries several hundred yards down the road, Julius and the others were whisked to a side road where they were transferred to another peasant's cart. The new driver took them across a field north of Ostrava, to the river. A small cabin boat carried them down river until they came to a designated farmhouse, where they spent the night.

A Lutheran minister and his wife, the host family, were eager to talk with their visitors. The minister asked Julius about conditions in Warsaw, but Julius was so tired that he could barely utter "It is worsening for Jews."

He was not interested in continuing the conversation. After a hearty meal, he excused himself and bedded down for the night.

The next morning the minister knocked on Julius's door before dawn. He called in, "Get up. We have breakfast for you before the next stage of your trip." The visitors were fed some rolls and coffee. They collected their bags, and the minister took them to a large horse driven coach owned by his church. The coach was used to convey travelers from Lithuania and Poland through a section of the Moravian low mountain range, heading toward Brunn.

A light rain was falling. The trip was treacherous because of the narrow, winding mountain roads. Once, while most of the passengers were napping, the coach skidded on the wet road and slid to the side. The two right wheels were mired in mud, and the waking passengers could see how precariously near the mountain edge the coach was situated.

The driver hollered for everyone to remain still. He asked Julius and two other men to slowly climb out of the coach, one by one, on the road side. They did so, while the rest of the passengers prayed and clasped each other. Two men pulled on the coach from the front and one, a fellow of great size, pushed from the rear. After several tries, the right wheels were dislodged from the mud and the coach was back on the road. The journey continued.

From Brunn they traveled to Vienna by cart. Compared with the previous mountain route, the flat roads made traveling relatively comfortable. At the Austrian border crossing they presented their passports and were cleared without incident.

The eight travelers were all Jewish, mostly middle aged or older. For all, America was their destination. Everyone appeared healthy, a necessity for the arduous trip as well as for entry to the United States. On the road they conversed from time to time, usually in Yiddish, mostly about their families and their fears about the long voyage ahead. It was night when they arrived in Vienna.

The coach passed through the city, gaily decorated for a celebration of the musical artistry the city was known for. Julius was enthralled with the bright lights and cheerful mood of those in the streets. It was in sharp contrast to what Warsaw had been when he left. Finally, the coach arrived at the railroad station.

He was extremely worn out, and worried that he would not have time to connect with the train to Paris. His train was scheduled to leave the next morning, and to make sure he would not miss it, he slept on a bench in the railway station He kept his belongings very close to him.

Julius was fascinated by the station architecture. He ran his eyes over the curved high ceilings. It was full of sculptural details—scenes of the city's history and statues of famous Viennese citizens. From his perspective on the bench, Julius could see the broad span and became absorbed in the detail. At last he drifted off.

In the middle of the night, he was shaken by a railway policeman. "No sleeping on the bench," he was told. He sat up, rubbed his face to stimulate it, and stood up and walked several times around the bench. "Thank you," he called to the policeman, who had already moved on and may not have heard him.

Julius gathered his things and looked for a cafe in the station, but everything was closed for the night. To stay awake, he wandered around the station until morning, waiting for his train to depart.

At last, his train was announced. He made his way to the track and boarded for Paris. Feeling confident about his ability to deal with railway inspectors from Austria and France, he relaxed and struck up conversations with other travelers. "Hello, where are you from?" "What are you reading?" He told a couple of jokes about German soldiers.

Some found him amusing while others were disturbed by his forward manner. When Julius realized he may be offending some of them, he stopped making remarks and remained quiet the rest of the trip. "I must not call attention to myself. If they find out I'm a Jew, they can make trouble for me."

When the train arrived in Paris, he was tempted to exit the station and see the city. He had heard so much about the many museums and gardens there. After thinking it over, he was afraid that something might happen to him that would prevent him from getting to America. Then he learned his train had come to Gare de L'Est in northeast Paris and the train to Boulogne would depart from Gare Montparnasse in the southeast part of the city. He took a horse drawn streetcar for the exchange. As a consequence, he got a peek at some of Paris.

After arriving in Boulogne, Julius checked into a boarding house he had been told about. On his second night there, he heard a disturbance in the main hallway just outside his room. He rushed out to find one of the other boarders lying on the rug. The manager of the house was bending over him. On seeing Julius, he cried out, "He collapsed. I don't know what's wrong with him. It will take at least an hour to get a doctor here."

Julius felt his pulse to make sure the man was still alive and then hurried back to his room to fetch the small bag in which he kept medical supplies. By that time, others had gathered in the area. None of them knew what to do but watched Julius administer to the ill man. The man opened his eyes and pointed to his throat. Julius first asked him to cough and then gave the boarder magnesia for indigestion. After a minute or so, the man smiled at Julius and said, "I feel much better."

The other boarders were impressed with Julius's medical skills and assumed he was a doctor. He did nothing to dispel their notion. "Get plenty of rest," he told his patient, "and don't eat too much rich food."

The morning the S. S. Netherlands was due to arrive in Boulogne, he got up early and went down to the pier with his luggage. When the ship arrived, he could see several passengers on the deck waving toward him and others on the pier. The time had come to cross the ocean to America.

CHAPTER 9

▼

The S.S. Netherlands was a clipper ship with three masts, one funnel, and a two cylinder compound steam engine driven by coal. It was built in Scotland in 1874. Three hundred and fifty feet long and thirty eight feet wide, its iron hull contributed heavily to its weight of 2,540 tons. During the last part of the nineteenth century, it was a frequent conveyor of Central and Eastern European emigrants to the United States and nearby areas. A Dutch owned ship, it usually departed from Rotterdam but often made a stop in Boulogne before continuing the long trek across the ocean. When filled, the Netherlands held fifty passengers in first and second class and as many as four hundred in third class (or steerage, as it was typically labeled). The ship had a crew of 47.

Abe and Rivka were excited as they boarded the S. S. Netherlands. It was the first ocean voyage for both of them. At last, they were truly headed for the United States.

The Captain and purser stood at the top of the gangplank to greet the arrivals. They nodded to the men and women and patted the heads of the children. All those boarding carried baggage of some type, some dragging large bags up the gangplank and others balancing smaller bags on their shoulders. Even youngsters helped bring their goods aboard.

Rivka wore one of the few dresses she took with her. It was not her best one but it fitted her well. Made of cotton, it was blue with patch pockets and fell to her ankles. A sash around her waist helped to outline her figure. Anticipating spells of cold air when they went on deck, her hair was covered with a kerchief, the same one she wore on the earlier trip from Libau to Amsterdam. Her inner spirit exuded happiness about going to America, but she was apprehensive about the voyage and acted a bit nervously.

Abe still had on the same suit he wore from the time he left Kraglova. It was dark blue and of his own making. It covered his generous figure quite well. He wore a white shirt he had washed at the transient hotel and a dark tie and black shoes. A fedora hat was perched on his head. He tried to be in command of himself and give an appearance of strength and calmness, but he too was anxious about the trip and wished it was already completed.

Rivka was carrying her cloth bag while Abe balanced his walk with his own suitcase in his left hand and Rivka's in his right hand.

Abe approached the Captain and asked him how long he thought it would take to get to New York.

"It depends mostly on the weather," answered the Captain. "We are expecting the voyage to take about two weeks. It's expected we will arrive in New York on May 23. Of course, it could be later or sooner, but we will get there. I hope you will enjoy the trip."

"Thank you," said Abe and, turning to Rivka, he remarked "Two weeks can be a long time but it will go by quickly if we keep thinking about seeing the statue of the woman in New York Harbor you told me about and our dear relatives."

Right behind them on the corridor leading to the sleeping quarters, an elderly couple were speaking German. Abe introduced himself and asked: "Are you going to join your family?"

"Yah, yah," was the reply.

Abe detected an unusual German accent and asked where they had lived.

"Munchen, Germany" said the old man.

"I once knew a family from Munchen. They were Jewish, however."

The elderly couple studied Abe and Rivka, and then the old man asked, "You are not Jews, are you?"

"Yes, we are," Rivka answered slowly. "We will be joining cousins in America."

The old man laughed. "We, too, are Jewish. We are going to join our children who are already in New York waiting for us. They went last year, and we've missed them a lot."

Crew members were assigned to escort each family to their quarters. One of the crew called out "Follow me" in his best German and led Rivka and Abe to different sections of steerage. Mothers, children, and unattached women were sent to one part and men to another. Some men objected to being separated from their families. One middle aged Polish man cried out "No, no" when he was shunted to the men's section. "My wife is pregnant and needs my help," he added. He only relented when he could see the separation applied to everyone, not just him, and the crewman told him a nurse would tend to his wife's needs.

The purser announced through a megaphone that ship's rules permitted meetings on deck during certain periods of the day. "The times will be posted in your area. Relax and make yourselves comfortable. And when the ship starts, stay in your beds. We don't want anyone falling down and getting hurt."

Steerage was far from an ideal place to spend the fourteen days expected for the trip. Some people occupied bunks stacked three high against a wall. Others, mostly children, had thin pallets on the floor. There was little room for belongings. The ship line made an effort to put people from the same country near each other, but most passengers found themselves almost shoulder to shoulder with fellow travelers from other nations whose language and customs were different from theirs.

"What a hellhole," said a stout Austrian man as he surveyed his quarters. "I know we didn't pay much money, but this is no way to treat people." Several men nodded their heads in accord.

"Momma, I don't like it here," said a small boy after he entered the compartment. "It's all right," said the mother. "The trip will be over before you know it, and you will get to see New York and your father."

Rivka had taken the lower bunk against one of the walls of the cubicle and had placed her suitcase and bag close by. She smiled at the children and nodded to the women in her area but refrained from engaging in conversation with any of them. She thought of her family back in Blutz and then of Abe in the other section. She wished the two of them could be closer to each other, but she understood the reason for separation. "I hope we have many opportunities to get together on the deck," she mused to herself.

The S. S. Netherland's foghorn blast caught everyone's attention and in a matter of minutes everyone felt some movement of the ship. Many tensed up and shut their eyes, while others strained to get some sort of view of the receding pier. "My stomach is rolling," commented an older Swedish woman. "I'm getting a headache in this close space," said a younger woman holding an infant.

Once underway, the ship swayed to and fro, the sails adjusting to the winds, the engines not powerful enough to effectively cut through the larger ocean currents. An older man began to vomit. He failed to reach the pots laid out for that purpose. A younger man took a shirt and waved it in front of the slits in the walls of the cubicles they occupied in steerage. It drew in some air but the stench and body odor was stronger than the ventilation.

Finally, the ship headed on a straight course. The purser told those in steerage they could go out on deck and watch as land disappeared. The more courageous among the travelers moved to the deck and held on to the rail. They were careful to avoid losing their footing and getting injured or thrown overboard. At this time, the ocean was fairly calm. One by one, other passengers made their way to the deck. "Look, look," said a Russian man, "We've already gone so far, you can't see where we left."

After about thirty minutes, the purser asked everyone to return to their sleeping area. They obeyed his direction and went down below to steerage.

Most of the travelers began to relax. "My stomach has settled down," said the Swedish woman. "Look at the birds flying around," shouted one of the boys who had managed to see the sky through one of the slits. "They're seagulls," his mother told him.

The passengers came from many countries in Europe—Holland, Germany, Poland, Sweden, France, Italy, and Switzerland, in addition to parts of Russia. So many languages made it difficult for Abe and Rivka to find others to talk to. Abe spoke German as well as Yiddish, Lithuanian, and a

Baltic language called Lettish. As a businessman, he had to learn several languages to deal with his customers. Rivka spoke the same languages but not as fluently as Abe. It was the Baltic and German travelers they could speak with most easily.

Abe was half asleep in his middle bunk. The night before at the hotel he awoke several times after bad dreams and his sleep was not very satisfying. He had two weeks to catch up on it. "Seeing Rivka on deck from time to time and spending the rest of my life with her fills my heart," he thought to himself.

After a couple of hours, with the ship sailing smoothly, the purser again allowed the passengers to go on deck. Abe was anxious to see Rivka and exchange stories about conditions in their respective quarters. After milling in the crowd for about ten minutes, they discovered each other and told their stories. They looked around for the German couple but couldn't find them.

After a short while, the ship's foghorn blasted and the Captain told the passengers to return to their compartments. Rivka and Abe separated after exchanging hugs. As she entered her steerage section, Rivka heard a woman's voice on the other side of her compartment. "This is awful," she was saying. "How can we live like this for a couple of weeks? Even in our village things were not this bad."

Most of the women seemed to be complaining about something. "I knew I should have brought a heavier coat. It could make the bed softer," said one. "Going on deck is the only pleasure we have," said another. Children were crying or screaming. Some mothers were wringing their hands and moaning. One said to her children, "Hush, hush, let me tell you some stories about your cousins in America." Rivka knew that sleep would be possible only when she could shut these distractions out of her mind.

When nightfall came, the Captain consented to let steerage passengers sleep on deck, where it was cool. The passengers swarmed out of their compartments and brought with them what heavier clothing and blankets they had. In no time, covered bodies spanned the inner portion of the deck. A man, happy to see his children, helped keep them warm by snuggling up to them. "Over here, over here," was heard from a woman whose daughter had gotten temporarily lost.

As daylight emerged, everyone was directed back to the steerage area. Family members embraced each other and said their goodbyes, hoping that before long a reunion would take place on deck.

On the second day out of Rotterdam, the ship entered the port of Boulogne. Whatever space was left was to be occupied by those boarding here. Many of those already on the ship went on deck to view the new arrivals.

When Julius boarded the ship at Boulogne late in the day, he discovered it to be nearly full. The bunks still unoccupied were the least favorable of all in the section. The Purser advised him where the spaces were located. He chose one and stored his bags in the small space provided. He fell into the lowest of a three tiered set of bunks.

There was little discussion among the travelers as the ship left the dock and headed out to deeper sea. Once the ship picked up speed and the helmsman turned the ship toward the ocean, there was some swaying from side to side and personal belongings kept on bunks fell to the floor from their insecure positions.

Some of the passengers were holding on to whatever they could grasp, bunk rails or a wall. Others were curled up in their bunks, a few putting their hands over their faces. Several small children leapt up from their pallets to be next to their mothers. Many looked at each other as if to say "What are we in for?"

After a spell, the ship stayed its course and people were adjusting to its motion. The passengers began to speak out. "Enough with the rolling already." "Can you believe twelve more days of this?" "It's all right now. Enjoy yourself while you can."

Julius looked up at the man occupying the bunk just above him and said, "Hello, I'm Julius Newman" in his best Polish. The man raised his hands as if to say "I don't understand you." Julius repeated his statement in Lithuanian. "Oh," said his bunkmate, "I am Abe Solomon, a tailor from Lithuania." Abe reached down to shake Julius's hand.

Abe asked how Julius had gotten to the ship. Julius recounted for Abe the complicated pathway he took to Boulogne. Abe, in turn, recalled his trip to Rotterdam.

There were dozens of men in their cubicle. Some were reading prayer books. Others were regaling each other with stories of their previous travels. A few had nodded off to sleep. One fellow in the far corner of the room was lying on a top bunk and staring into space. Whenever Abe looked his way, the man was in the same position. Abe signaled Julius and pointed toward the man. The fear was that he might have died. Julius said "Let me check his pulse." Before he reached him, the man moved his left arm and then resumed his stare.

A member of the crew arrived with a large pot of soup and dark bread. Each of the passengers was given a wooden bowl and spoon and a ladle of soup with a sliver of bread. "That's all I get?" asked Abe. The crewman looked at him and promptly moved on to the next person. "They don't want you to get too fat," said a voice a few bunks away.

When darkness descended on the ship, there was very little light to read by or to see each other in steerage. Abe told Julius: "I'll try to get some sleep. I'm not sure I can do it with the noise from the ship and the people here." Julius pulled out a wad of cotton from his coat pocket. He separated it into four pieces and gave two to Abe. "Here," he said, "stuff these in your ears. It will drown out the noise."

After a night of fitful sleep and a breakfast of more bread and soup, the men lined up to use the two toilets in the cubicle. Everyone was stirring in anticipation of the time to go on deck. Abe told Julius about Rivka being on the ship but didn't reveal his relationship to her. Julius showed the small pouch in his bag where he kept pharmaceutical items he felt would be helpful on the trip. "A few days ago," he said, "I was dispensing these to my customers and now I am keeping them in readiness for myself."

Abe pulled out a suit he was tailoring for himself. With great pride he explained how he stitched the cloth to make it something special. "You don't find quality like this in most clothing shops in Lithuania." Julius told of writing his family about his arrival, and Abe said he expected his cousins would be in New York waiting for him.

When the time came for the sexes to intermingle on the deck, Abe told Julius, "You'll get to meet my cousin now." Men, women, and children rushed to the deck in a tumultuous flow. It was hard to spot Rivka for a while. When Abe found her, he introduced her to Julius.

The people were so bunched up together it was hard to observe anyone's clothes and bodily appearance, but Rivka was radiant and many of the men were staring at her. A few made suggestive remarks. She acted pleased but didn't reply to any comments. Julius, in particular, was attracted to her, despite her obviously older age, and told jokes intended to make her laugh. Rivka enjoyed his company. Abe was not pleased by all the attention to his cousin.

When Abe went back to steerage to use the toilet he'd passed up earlier because of the long line, Rivka and Julius remained on deck for a while. They were the last to return to their quarters after the ship's purser signaled the end of the deck visitation period.

Abe didn't get back to the deck before the time was up. When Julius got to the cubicle, he told Abe how attractive and interesting his cousin was. Abe told him what Rivka and he had arranged before the trip began. Julius congratulated him but said, "Women can be unpredictable. Tomorrow she may have a change of mind."

A few days passed and the ship was on course for a timely arrival in New York. Many passengers had adjusted to the difficulties of the voyage. But some men were still upset by conditions of steerage and complained loudly to anyone who would hear them.

Julius's beard now covered his face. Looking into a small mirror he had in his bag, he acted pleased with the way it had developed. "Maybe I should have done this a long time ago," he murmured to himself. "I might have had more women admire me."

Rivka looked forward to the few times each day when she could join Abe and Julius. She had not made any friends among the women, although she had introduced herself to one of her bunkmates. She spent her days in her compartment squinting in the dark area while she mended a dress she hoped to wear for the New York landing.

The first few days of the trip she was feeling well. Late on the fifth day she told a woman in the bunk just above her she was ailing. "It's probably just an upset stomach," she said.

Julius had brought along a deck of playing cards and a small checker set. When they got bored, Abe and Julius played *pisha paysha*, a Russian card game, or checkers. Neither of the men was an astute player at checkers; however, it didn't require a lot of brain power and they could talk while playing. The games were mostly friendly. Abe did become irritated when Julius beat him easily several times.

"You must play this a lot," he said, sulking.

"No, very seldom," said Julius.

"That's enough. I'd like to get back to my sewing."

One of the other male passengers told his bunkmate he'd heard Abe and Julius arguing a couple of times. He said: "Whether it was about a game or something else I don't know. Once I heard Abe say something about his cousin."

Six or seven days of the voyage stretched ahead. More of the passengers were becoming ill as a storm caused the ship to roll more than usual. Some of the children became afraid and were calmed by their mothers, who themselves were disturbed. "Be still," said one of the mothers as she looked around with a fearful face. The storm finally let up and the ship assumed its prior bearing.

A crewman brought bread, cheese, and figs to the passengers for a mid day meal. Some of the Jews discussed the appropriateness of eating what was brought to them. The oldest among the men remarked: "If we were home, we would not eat some of these things. But what choice do we have if we want to survive?" The others agreed with him, some reluctantly. "When we get to New York, I can be a good Jew again," said one of them.

In the other steerage section, two of the women began arguing. One, a stout Italian woman, claimed the other, a short, thin French woman, had encroached on her space. "We hardly have room to breathe," she said. "Don't push your bags into my place." A third woman, who was Dutch, attempted to intervene. "Look, the trip is miserable enough without creating new problems. We have to get along with each other if we want to make it to New York." The complaining woman nodded her head. The other one pulled her belongings closer to the place she was occupying.

Rivka continued to feel ill and remained in her bunk while others went out on deck and then returned after about twenty minutes.

A subsequent deck visit was canceled because of a storm, making many of the passengers feel especially constrained. Before it was time for the next visit to the deck, a crew member reported to the Captain, "Many of the passengers are shouting to go on deck even if it is not now the scheduled time." The Captain relented and ordered the purser to permit the passengers to spend a short period on deck. It was near the end of the day and darkness was approaching. Most passengers came on deck. When it was time to go back to their cubicles, the purser told them to wait a while and he then disappeared. Half an hour later, they were told by a crewman they could return to their quarters.

Some time later, several of the passengers told their neighbors about hearing the voice of the Captain giving orders, as well as the footsteps of scurrying crew members. Others listened and confirmed the sounds. The noise continued for several minutes and the passengers talked among themselves. The man who slept in the bunk above Abe's, usually very quiet, told those around him: "I haven't seen the men below me since we came back from the deck."

At the same time, one of the women in the other section said: "I haven't seen Rivka since we came back in."

"She's not in the toilet," said another. "I just went there. I know she wasn't feeling well when we went on deck."

A couple of the men peered through the slits in their cubicle to see what was going on. They tried to listen to the conversation taking place outside.

The one who could hear best said, "The Captain gave orders to the crew to wrap bodies in blankets and tie ropes around them to bind the coverings. He commanded: 'Be careful! Make sure the ropes are tight.' I could barely see four of the crew take the wrapped bodies and lower them over the side of the ship. 'Drop them slowly,' I heard the Captain say."

A Dutchman told others: "I, too, had a good view from the slit near my bunk. I am sure I heard the Captain talking with the purser. I believe the

Captain was instructing the purser not to record what happened until the ship arrived in New York. I can't be certain, though. Part of what he was saying was hard to hear."

Rumors spread around the steerage area. The male passengers become more nervous. "Something strange is going on here," said one of them. One of the married men managed to get out of his cubicle and crawl over to the women's section and call out to his wife: "Maria, are you there? Have you heard what just happened?" "No," she said. He told her and she passed the word along to the other women. They were all frightened. One of the women put her hand to her face and cried out, "My God, was one of those bodies Rivka's?"

The ship continued its course toward New York.

CHAPTER 10

▼

(In New York after relatives were told their loved ones had died)

At the suggestion of the ship line officials, Sarah Newman and Sheyna Goetz planned to meet with the Captain of the S. S. Netherlands. They needed to know what had taken place on the ship. They wanted to know how their relatives had died.

Sheyna, still very distraught, arranged for a neighbor to look after her children so she could go with Sarah. She would write to the families in the old country to tell them what had happened.

Sarah got permission from her boss to leave work to see the Captain. Her boss was kind, although it was costing her lost wages to search for answers to the mystery of the deaths at sea.

Sarah had agreed to stop by to get Sheyna so they could go together to the hotel where the Captain was staying. Sheyna lived on the fourth floor of a six story tenement. Sarah climbed the stairs and found the apartment, where Sheyna was waiting for her and welcomed her. The two women hugged each other and their eyes were still swollen from crying.

The dwelling had three small rooms and was in the rear of the building. Two of the rooms were dark and the third had one window in the upper part of a wall. That was all the natural light the apartment could receive. The rooms were cluttered with all the belongings of the family, and two beds were shared by Sheyna's entire family. Her husband worked the night shift at a factory and he slept in the daytime when most of the family was away. An air shaft separated the dwellings and a narrow hallway outside the apartment led to the common toilets.

The tenements—the densely occupied, multi story buildings that were packed in a few wards on the Lower East Side—did not first come into being with the recent wave of immigration. Early in the nineteenth century, when German and Irish immigrants came to New York, rows of single family residences in the Wall Street and Cherry Hill districts of the East Side were demolished to make way for multiple dwelling units to accommodate the new arrivals.

As immigration continued, the demand for housing led to more of these units and they spread to other areas of lower Manhattan. Their proximity to each other and inadequate facilities created accumulation of filth and a high risk of contagious diseases. It was not until 1867 that a Tenement House Act was passed that set standards for fire escapes, toilets per capita, and sewer connections, but insufficient funds were provided for their implementation.

A dozen years later a so called "dumbbell" design of tenement was the mode of construction. It was built on a lot 25 feet wide by 100 feet or less deep, with apartments for four families in each of five or six stories. A stairway in the center of the building reduced the width of middle rooms, generally bedrooms for several people, to no more than nine feet. The narrow light and airshaft further lessened the floor space of the middle rooms. Light and air were at a premium in some of the rooms. Since many families accepted boarders to help pay the rent, the number of people in a building could amount to 150 or more.

This was the type of place that Sheyna and her family occupied.

"You should excuse the appearance," said Sheyna. "It's not yet cleaned up today. With all the *tsauros*, I haven't kept up with my duties."

Sheyna got her coat and the two women descended the stairway to the street level. They decided to walk to the Captain's hotel. It was over a mile, but the weather was good and the walk gave them a chance to talk privately.

"This has been a nightmare," Sarah said. "Just this morning we were waiting to welcome our relatives to America and show them what a wonderful place it is. Now, we have to find out what went wrong."

"I'm worried about my Irving," Sheyna said. "Such a good boy. He wanted to take his cousins around New York, to show them everything. He wanted to hear them tell stories of life in the old country. This was a great shock for him. I hope it doesn't mix up his head. My other boys are young enough they will soon forget what happened. And I have trouble writing letters to Rivka's family and Abe's cousins still in Lithuania. It is so hard to tell them."

They crossed over to Orchard Street. Pushcarts lined the sidewalks and men and women were hawking their wares. A man in his twenties, with a load of coats draped over his shoulders, stepped in front of them. "I've got beautiful coats for you, and the price is very cheap. Look at this one. Isn't it fine? Your friends would be jealous of you." The women shook their heads and moved on.

"Hey, lady," a young boy called to Sarah. "Buy a bagel from me. It's just two pennies." Sarah waved him off.

They turned the corner toward East Broadway, where there would be fewer sellers on the street. They then headed north to 24th Street.

The modest, somewhat seedy hotel where they found the captain stood on 24th Street off Eighth Avenue. A sign above the front door read HOTEL ESPLANADE in faded letters. If Sarah had gone there alone, she might have been mistaken for a prostitute. The presence of the older, more matronly Sheyna would lead observers to assume they were a mother and daughter.

They asked at the hotel desk for the captain's room number. The clerk asked, "Is he expecting you?" "Yes," replied Sarah, "but we hadn't set a time." The clerk directed them to a dirty looking elevator. They got in, closed the gate and were lifted to the second floor. They made their way down the dark, grimy hall to 214.

Gingerly, Sarah knocked on the door. It was opened by a large man, maybe six feet tall and heavy set. He was wearing an official ship uniform with baggy pants and an ill fitting jacket decorated with various insignias.

His face was ruddy and his reddish brown hair was parted in the middle. A long spindly mustache drooped down over his pockmarked face.

The ship line officials had informed him that the surviving families would be coming to see him. As he looked at his visitors, he managed a half smile but quickly changed it to a studied expression of concern.

"Come in, please," he said, as he waved his right hand toward the worn furniture in the entry room. "I am Harald Meergossen. My official title is Ship Master, but everyone calls me Captain."

"I am Sarah Newman and this is Sheyna Goetz. We've come to talk about my brother and her cousins."

"Please, please, sit." His English was fluent but his Dutch accent modified every word. The women settled into the upholstered chairs and the Captain brought a straight backed wooden chair close to where they were sitting.

"Thank you for meeting with us." Sarah then started to explain what they wanted to know. The mood was tense and tears began to well in Sheyna's eyes. The women became more relaxed when they sensed the Captain seemed to be a gentle man and sincere about assisting them.

As Sarah began, "Sir, what we want to know…," the Captain cut her off in mid sentence and begged her to allow him to describe the situation.

"Ladies, first let me say what an awful thing has happened and I am very sorry," the Captain began. "I have been a ship master for 24 years. I've often crossed the Atlantic each way. Many times we carried passengers to America. Traveling by ship is always a hazardous thing."

He leaned toward them, elbows on his knees. "I cannot remember a single voyage when there was not some type of problem. Sometimes bad weather creates difficulties. Sometimes there are mechanical failures aboard. Sometimes the passengers have never been on a ship before and cannot adjust to the experience.

"Of course, you want to learn about your own people. But I wanted to give some background for the recent unfortunate happening. This is a dangerous world we live in."

Sarah shifted nervously in her chair. Mrs. Goetz was dabbing her eyes with her handkerchief.

"Well, the fact is that your brother, Miss Newman, and your cousins, Mrs. Goetz, were victims of cholera. It is a very deadly disease. We try to screen passengers for health problems before they board. Usually, we can spot illnesses, and the sick person is not allowed to aboard." He leaned back and rubbed his eyes.

"We have a nurse on the ship who tends to passengers' health concerns. She examines them if they say they are ill or others suspect it. She isn't a doctor, but she has many years of experience.

"A woman passenger told the nurse that Miss Borchowitz was very ill. When the nurse examined her, she was in shock and dehydrated. Her face was blue, her eyes sunk into her head, and her lips were cracked."

Sheyna moaned and shook her head from side to side. Sarah reached out to her to comfort her.

The Captain went on: "The nurse had seen this many times and recognized that she had cholera. She put Miss Borchowitz in a sick room we managed to save for such situations, but people with cholera have not much chance of surviving without a doctor or the right medicines.

"The purser quickly checked the ship manifest and saw that she had boarded with Mr. Solomon. He rushed to the men's section and found Mr. Solomon and Mr. Newman in their bunks, both ill with the same symptoms. They were also placed in the sick room."

Sheyna shook her head again and more tears flowed.

"How awful," Sarah said, her face showing anguish.

"I'm afraid it was too late. Nothing could be done. They died within minutes of each other. Awful, awful. As a captain I have to do my duty. According to the rules, if a passenger dies at sea, we wrap the body in a blanket and put it into the sea. We must do this."

Sarah and Sheyna had been listening attentively, but they had questions. "Is cholera often a problem on your ship?" asked Sarah.

"It happens from time to time, though we try to prevent it. That's why we examine passengers for illness before they can board. It's a problem in Russia and Poland and other countries. When people travel and migrate, they spread the disease. Last August in Hamburg, there was a major epidemic. Many ships leave there to come to America."

"But why on a ship to America?" Sarah asked.

"The ship agents told me a few hundred Russian Jews on the Lower East Side of New York were diagnosed with cholera soon after their arrival. They passed it on to relatives who already lived here. They said the captain of the S.S. Moravia reported that passengers on his ship coming to America toward the end of last year died from cholera. We thought the typhus fever epidemic of a year ago was bad, but cholera is much worse. What can I say? Health conditions are improving but not fast enough."

"So how many others on your ship got cholera and died too?" Sarah asked. "I didn't hear the officials on the dock mention anyone else."

The Captain cleared his throat and coughed a few times. "Excuse me. I think maybe I am getting a cold. But never mind. Your question. No, others were sick on the ship, but no one else had the cholera symptoms. We were able to bring the rest of the passengers to America. It is sometimes a strange thing. Your three people may have been together before coming to the ship, or they came from the same area. I don't know. When the Port of Immigration Medical Examiner finishes his investigation, we will get a report. Then maybe we'll know better.

"I wish it were otherwise. Nothing pleases me more than seeing our passengers rejoining families and friends. I know, especially for the Jews, coming to America is a God send. Everyone has heard about the pogroms they have been through. Please extend my heartfelt sympathy to your families." Rising, he moved toward the door.

Sheyna put her hand on his arm. "Rivka and Abe were cousins. They lived not so far from each other. But Sarah's brother came from Warsaw, far away from those two. Also, he boarded the ship in France, the other two in Rotterdam. Why them? Why not others?"

"Of course, you raise a good question," said the Captain. "But if any one was ill and was friendly with the others, that could explain it. And maybe they didn't talk much with others. It was only a couple of days after we left Boulogne that this tragedy occurred. I don't have the answer. But these things happen."

"My brother was a pharmacist," Sarah interjected. "He should have recognized the symptoms. They must have suffered terribly, even if only for a short time."

"Yes, yes, it was terrible." said the captain.

The two women turned toward each other and Sarah moved over to embrace Sheyna. Tears flowed freely.

"These were good people who wanted to make new lives in America," said Sarah. "We hadn't seen my brother for nearly two years. You can't imagine how this has upset my parents. It is unbelievable to think that Julius would be a victim of cholera. Why, why?"

The Captain nodded his head. "It hurts me to have to tell you about it, but it is my duty to report what took place."

Sarah and Sheyna thanked the Captain for talking with them. "We would like to see the report you mentioned. Can you see that we are notified when it is ready?" asked Sarah.

"Write your address here," said the Captain, "and I will see that you get the report."

As a last thought, Sarah asked him where they could find the purser and the nurse.

"I can't tell you where the nurse is now. She won't be going back on my ship. The purser is in New York until our return trip but I don't know where. Ask at the port office. I don't think he knows anything more than what I have just told you."

The women headed home, mulling over the Captain's words. They believed what he told them but something still puzzled them. Why did just those three out of hundreds get an infectious disease and not give it to others? They agreed on one thing. They wanted to talk with the purser.

It had been a long Tuesday. The women were tired as they walked toward their homes. Sarah had so much she still wanted to do, but it was getting late and she would have to wait till the next day.

"In the morning I'll make an inquiry at the ship line office," she said.

At Sheyna's home, they said their farewells. When Sheyna told Sarah she could not accompany her the next day, Sarah assured her it was all right. She promised to keep Sheyna informed if she learned anything more. Sarah headed home to report the sad findings to her parents.

CHAPTER 11

▼

When Sarah awoke Wednesday morning, she was determined to find the purser and the nurse. She wanted to know more about what happened on the ship. She knew it would be difficult to find them. Time was of the essence. The purser would be in New York for only a few days, up to the time for the S. S. Netherlands to return to Rotterdam.

Sarah's boss had been kind and sympathetic, but he needed her in the office. She had missed a day already. Sarah feared losing her job. But this was important. "One more day," she pleaded with her boss.

Sarah followed the Captain's suggestion and went back to the ship registry office. The man at the desk remembered her from the day before. Sarah asked about the purser's location. At first he hesitated but then he relented: "I'm not supposed to do this," he said, "but I guess this is a special case."

Looking at a record book, he referred to a note on one of the pages. "You can try 903 West 51st Street. That's an apartment building on the west side. Look for the name Naflick."

"Is that the purser's name?" asked Sarah."

"No, it's LaFontaine" replied the clerk, "Anthony LaFontaine. He's Belgian."

Sarah thanked him and left. She sat down on one of the nearby benches. Hungry, she remembered that she hadn't eaten breakfast. Sarah reached down in her bag to see if part of yesterday's pastry was still there.

It wasn't. She then remembered she had thrown the remains away. She strolled over to an area where an old man was selling hot chestnuts and bought a bagful. She nibbled on a few to satisfy her stomach.

Anxiously, Sarah took the horse trolley to 51st Street. She then walked across several intersections till she came to a brick building marked 903. It was already mid morning. Inside the door were mailboxes with the names of the tenants. She spotted Naflick, and walked up one flight to apartment 10.

A woman answered the knock at the door.

"I'm Sarah Newman. I was told that Mr. LaFontaine might be here. I have urgent business about his ship."

The woman looked her over carefully and said, "Just a minute."

Shortly, a slim, rather short, man with a tanned complexion, presented himself. He seemed puzzled by the appearance of the visitor and asked in English with a French accent, "Do I know you?"

Sarah identified herself and indicated her purpose for being there. She didn't mention having seen the Captain.

LaFontaine, appearing somewhat ill at ease, said, "Oh, yes, please come in." He gestured for Sarah to sit and sat across from her. "Yes, a terrible situation. It is always a tragedy when a passenger dies on the ship. Almost always it cannot be avoided, and this was certainly such a case."

Sarah asked "Would it have made a difference if a doctor had been on board?"

"No," LaFontaine said, clearly measuring his words. He went on, "The poison worked quickly and if a doctor was present, he probably would not have had the correct antidote."

Sarah looked stunned. It was clear that the Captain and the purser had not spoken to each other since the ship docked. Evidently the purser believed his account of what happened on the ship. He spoke it with conviction.

LaFontaine continued, "I have seen romances develop on ships many times and I have also observed two men having interests in the same woman from time to time. Usually this doesn't amount to much. A flirtation, maybe even an embrace takes place."

He nodded his head several times to punctuate what he was saying. "I notice these things. You know I am responsible for the welfare of passengers on the ship, so I keep an eye on what is going on aboard ship. Of course, I am not a priest or a policeman and I try not to be a judge of morals. Yet, nothing that takes place on board should threaten the well being of the passengers. I can see to that."

"What are you saying?" interrupted Sarah. "Was there some conflict between Julius and other passengers that led to his death?" She had a puzzled look on her face. She shifted in her chair.

"Oh," replied the purser, "there was something going on among the three of them—your brother and the man and woman he befriended and later killed. Miss Borchowitz and Mr. Solomon were his victims, and he did himself in. A very troubling situation, I am sorry to say."

Sarah recoiled in horror.

"It doesn't make sense," said Sarah, her lips quivering. "My brother was a gentle person. He would never harm anyone."

"Ah," retorted LaFontaine, "He was a pharmacist, yes?"

Sarah acknowledged that he was and asked "Why, what difference does that make?"

The purser lit a cigarette and continued talking. "Your brother had with him a small bag with different medicines from his apothecary. He told us they were for maintaining his own health—medicines for headaches, seasickness, and the sort. What we later discovered was that his bag also contained some strychnine. The very poisonous colorless crystals look harmless, but they are capable of killing people."

"That's possible." said Sarah. "My father is also a pharmacist and I know about strychnine. Doctors sometimes prescribe it in small doses for the nervous system. I know that Julius was a good pharmacist and only used medicines properly. It is possible that he had been having problems with his own nervous system and brought it along for his own use."

"Well," said LaFontaine, "that may be true, but that's not what he did in this situation."

"What do you mean?" Sarah asked.

"Your brother was paying a lot of attention to Miss Borchowitz. She was a little older but an attractive woman, and I understood not married. She seemed not to mind the attention and spoke with him frequently. We were told that Mr. Solomon was related to Miss Borchowitz and he was looking out for her. He, too, seemed infatuated with her. He seemed jealous of the time your brother and Miss Borchowitz were together. On our third day out of port, some deck hands heard the two men arguing. No blows, but they were loud and very angry.

"Another passenger later told me, when a meal was being served on deck and the three were sitting together, Miss Borchowitz urged them to remain friends. Not very much later, she and Mr. Solomon became violently ill. They were choking and gasping. The nurse was called and tried to administer to them but soon they were dead.

The nurse examined them and said that she had seen such a thing happen before—from poisoning by strychnine. Mr. Solomon had taken some sweet pudding and he gave Miss Borchowitz a taste of it. It made them both sick.

"I was told your brother was shocked. I surmised he meant the strychnine for Solomon, not Miss Borchowitz. When your brother saw Miss Borchowitz become ill, he understood what he had done. He was later found in his bed. He took some of the poison himself. That's where the nurse found him."

Sarah kept shaking her head from side to side. "I still can't believe it." Tears welled in her eyes and she buried her head in her hands.

The purser stood for a moment and then sat back down. A period of silence ensued, after which the purser commented, "Who knows what tempts people to do things in some circumstances they wouldn't do in others?

"If your brother had never met Miss Borchowitz or Mr. Solomon. If he had been placed in another part of steerage. Then maybe life would have gone on as before and these three would be with their relatives now."

As she began to collect herself, Sarah tried to contemplate the circumstance that would have driven Julius to commit such an act. She was incredulous that her own brother would engage in criminal behavior, and such a form of crime that violated not only the law but also the code of his profession.

She asked LaFontaine about Julius's bag with the remaining strychnine. "Was it turned over to authorities?"

The purser told her he and the Captain had decided it was best to dispose of the poison. They didn't want it to get into anyone else's hands, so they threw the container in the ocean. He then repeated what the Captain said about how the bodies of the deceased were covered with blankets and thrown into the sea. "That," he said, "is common practice when a passenger dies and the ship is far from a port."

Sarah was upset by what she had just learned. Preparing to leave, she asked him, "Can you tell me where I can find the ship's nurse?"

LaFontaine answered, "No, I really don't know."

Sarah left the apartment still in a stupor. It was shortly after noon. She started to walk slowly back to her home. She needed to give herself time to think things through. Absentmindedly, she headed off in the wrong direction. After going one block, she realized her mistake and headed the right way.

Now she had two versions of what took place on ship, two distinctly different stories. Which one was the real story?

She ran the two scenarios through her head, over and over.

The Captain seemed honest and responsible. He knew about the cholera outbreaks in Russia and Poland and recently in Hamburg. It was very possible that only these three got the disease, and it was maybe luck that others on the ship weren't infected. But perhaps the Captain didn't want to reveal the true story about the love triangle and poisoning and substituted the report of cholera deaths.

The purser's story was hard to accept. She found it hard to believe that her brother could commit such a criminal act. But, if they had really died of cholera, why didn't the purser say this? Why would he present such a different, and disturbing, account? And he spoke with such confidence.

Sarah would have to tell her family and the Goetzes what the purser said. She braced herself. It had been hard enough to tell them her brother was dead. Now she would have to tell her parents their son may have been a murderer.

CHAPTER 12

▼

With the afternoon sun beating down, Sarah made her way toward her apartment. When she got off the trolley, she caught a glimpse of her neighbor, Mrs. Cohen. Molly had spotted her the previous day at the pier when they were all waiting for the ferries.

"Mrs. Cohen, Mrs. Cohen," Sarah called out.

As she approached, she asked, "Wasn't that you at the pier yesterday?"

"Yes, I was there."

"Who were you waiting for?"

"We were meeting my sister and her family, from Lithuania. We're so grateful they got out of that country. Now they can live life in peace and freedom."

Sarah thought for a moment and then asked, "Was it the S. S. Netherlands they came on?"

"Yes, that was the ship. My sister's right upstairs. Why don't you come up and meet her?"

Sarah agreed but first felt it necessary to tell Mrs. Cohen what had happened to her brother and Sheyna's cousins. She said nothing, though, of the information she got from the Captain and purser about how the deaths occurred.

"How terrible! I know how much your parents were looking forward to his coming. What a tragedy!" Mrs. Cohen said. "Maybe my sister, Lena, knows something. Her husband and their children were also on the ship. They said it wasn't too pleasant, but they survived."

In the apartment, introductions were made. "Lena and Max Levin. Please meet one of my neighbors, Sarah Newman. Her parents are good friends.

"Here, Sarah, have some of my fresh *taglach* and tea." The Levin children, Sammy and Rachel, each had one of the honey balls.

The recent arrivals had little command of English but Sarah was able to converse with them in Yiddish. After an exchange of niceties, Sarah asked if they knew about any deaths that occurred on their ship.

At mention of the deaths, Lena and Max glanced at each other. "Tut, tut, tut," said Lena. It was as if they were eager to speak about it but were unsure as to what they should say. Lena reached out her hand to grasp Max's.

Mrs. Cohen, sensing their reluctance to comment, remarked, "It's okay. You're in America now. You can say what you want. No soldiers or police will arrest you for it. Sarah is a good neighbor. Tell her if you know anything."

Max, in his forties, maybe five foot eight, with a swarthy complexion and a dark stubble on his face, began by talking about all the difficulties they had in making arrangements for the voyage and in making their way to Rotterdam. He went into great detail about every step along the way— false train tickets they had received for one leg of the journey, mishaps on the train, their inadequate accommodations in Rotterdam, their daughter's terrible cold and how they were concerned that they would be prevented from boarding the ship. "But," he said, "the important thing is that we're now here. *Got tsu danken!*"

Lena Levin had remained quiet while her husband was speaking, but as soon as he finished his remarks she caught his eye and received a nod from him indicating she could say something.

She was typical of the traditional Eastern European *shtetl* woman. Her dark hair was drawn back and twisted into a bun at the back of her head. There was no makeup on her face. Her dress was simple and long, and she wore heavy brown stockings and plain brown shoes. She sat rigidly, her knees tightly together.

"I was most concerned about the children," Lena said. "We wanted to make sure they survived, so they could grow up to be fine citizens of the United States, with a good education."

"But on the ship," asked Sarah, "were you treated well? And did you notice if other persons on the ship were also treated well?"

Max told the children to go in the other room and play.

"Let me tell you," Lena said, "We knew it wouldn't be a picnic, but the sailors on the boat were not nice. In fact, I'll say they were evil people."

Sarah asked for further explanation.

Lena, again looking toward Max before continuing, said, "When they didn't have a job to do they roamed around and bothered people. All the women complained about being touched in private places. These sailors felt they could have anything they wanted and who could object. Where we come from, you don't touch women like that. These men had no manners, and nobody stopped them, not the Captain, not the purser, no one."

"Did you complain to the Captain?"

"What good would it do to complain? He couldn't handle them any better than we could. If Max had said anything, they would have beaten him. That happened to another man on the ship."

That comment disturbed Sarah, so she asked again: "What about the three people who died on the ship? Do you know what happened to them? Were they sick from a disease or from some food or from something else? I need to know because one of them was my brother."

Max and Lena together said "Ach, we're very sorry to hear that."

They glanced at each other again. Once more Max nodded that it was all right for Lena to say more. After sipping her tea a couple of times. Lena shook her head and uttered "The beasts!"

"What do you mean? Who are the beasts?"

"Let me tell you a story." Lena said. "One evening on the ship, right after we were allowed to go on deck, a woman named Rivka—she was sleeping near me and my children—went back to her bed. We heard a terrible scream, very loud. It was a woman's scream. I thought it was Rivka.

We were all too afraid to go back to our quarters because who knows what could happen to us.

"Then two men who had been with Rivka on the deck raced to the women's quarters. Soon we heard a big commotion. The Captain and purser, and some of the sailors, hurried to our area. After a while, the noise died down, but some people heard the Captain talking and the purser making some comments too.

"The people on deck were told to stay there until they were given permission to go to their beds. My children were getting tired and needed to go to sleep. But what could we do? We waited until we were told we could go below.

"Many of us looked around when we went back but we didn't see Rivka. We didn't see the men either. Maybe one of them was your brother."

Sarah had been glued to her seat and straining to catch every word Lena spoke. Mrs. Cohen put her hand over her mouth.

"We wanted to know what went on, but we knew it was better to keep quiet," continued Lena. "Of course, the women kept whispering and gossiping. Someone thought one of the sailors had raped Rivka. But no one saw anything.

Lena looked over at Max again, and went on.

"Then, one woman who had stayed on the deck a little longer than the rest of us, because she said she needed more air, came into our section. She looked pale. 'Have you heard?' she asked. We shook our heads. 'What is it?'

"This woman sat down on a bunk. She said she overheard a conversation between the Captain and the purser. Three sailors had gone into the women's area to look for things they could steal. When they got to Rivka's spot, they saw a bag that was bulging. They opened it up and took out some silver pieces.

"Next, Rivka came back and argued with them. One of the sailors banged her head against a post. That must have been when we heard the scream. It must have injured her head and she was dead right away. When the two men who raced there saw what had happened, they began to fight with the sailors, but they had nothing to fight with except their hands. The sailors stabbed them to death."

Mrs. Cohen gave a short shriek. Sarah looked horrified.

"Well," Lena said, coming to sit closer to Sarah, "we were all afraid they would come back and steal from us or maybe even harm us too. So from that time on, we were all careful. Later, when I told Max this story, he was furious but he didn't want to make a fuss. He knew the sailors might hurt him next." Max nodded his head.

"A little later, a few of us heard people moving around on the deck and what seemed like splashes in the water. We put two and two together and decided that the story we heard was true and the bodies were being tossed overboard. It was frightening.

"After seeing Cossacks riding on horses and swinging their bayonets to cut off the heads or arms of Jews in the old country, this was not unusual—but this was on a ship going to America, not in a ghetto in Russia."

"Didn't anyone say something to the Captain?" Sarah asked.

"Well, some of the women talked about it quietly, but for the rest of the trip nothing more was said about this night, and we didn't hear of anything like that taking place again.

"But you can imagine how happy we were when the ship docked here and we got to Ellis Island. What a relief! I am still shaking. We thank God we are now here with my sister. We want to be safe here. We want a new life."

Sarah could not believe what she had heard. She moved over and hugged Lena. "What a frightening experience. And my brother gone. It's hard to realize."

She then looked directly into Lena's face and asked her, "Did you see any of this yourself? How do you know that the story the other woman told you was true?"

Lena hesitated and then spoke. "Well, no, I didn't actually see or hear anything myself, but I believed that woman. She said she heard Rivka scream. We believed her. We all knew what beasts those sailors were."

Sarah thought about what Lena had told her.

Sarah now had heard a third version of how her brother and Sheyna's cousins had died. This story was just as possible as the other two, but Lena said she heard the story from another woman who claimed to have listened in on a conversation between the Captain and the purser. She did hear a splash though, so the bodies were thrown overboard.

Sarah could see that Lena was an emotional person and under a lot of stress. From what she said, perhaps she too had been bothered by the sailors. Perhaps her story was her way of getting back at them, at least in her own mind. Sarah found this story believable as well.

"Thank you for telling this to me," Sarah said. "I know it was difficult for you to talk about such an experience."

Turning to her neighbor, Sarah said, "Mrs. Cohen, how lucky you are to have your sister and her family here now."

"I prayed for over a year that Lena and Max and the children would come here," said Mrs. Cohen. "They had to get away from Russia, even if it meant they were leaving the place where generations of the family had lived."

Max and Lena again expressed their sorrow at Julius' death.

Sarah left the apartment and headed home. What would she say to her heart broken family?

Sarah recited the three stories for her family. At dinnertime, no one had an appetite for food. Sarah told her parents and her visiting sister, Feyga, she wanted to see her friend Molly for a little while. "I'll be back in less than an hour."

Molly lived a block and a half away and Sarah got to her place in a matter of minutes. "Can you take a stroll?" she asked her friend. "I have to tell you what happened today."

"I'm all confused," Sarah said. "After Sheyna and I talked to the Captain, we thought we knew all there was to know. Now there are three explanations of what happened to Julius and the others." She told them to Molly. "How can we know the truth now? We can't leave it like this. It's important to my family and, I'm sure, to Sheyna's to know the truth."

"What you need is someone to help you," commented Molly, "and I know someone I think would be just right. His name is Albert Gordon.

He's a lawyer, and he's helped other immigrants and their families. I met him at the "Y" once, before I met you. I was attending his lecture there and we spoke afterward. People were asking him questions about immigrant problems."

"How can we find him?"

"Wait. A man who lives in my apartment is a lawyer. He might have a list of lawyers in New York City and can tell us where Albert's office is located."

"If he can tell us that, we can send a note by messenger to Albert's office in the morning, and tell him we will come by tomorrow right after work."

"Great idea. Now, let's go to my apartment house and find my lawyer neighbor."

Within minutes Molly was knocking at Howard Goski's door. He answered it himself. "Hello." he said to Molly. "Don't you live upstairs?"

"Yeah," said Molly, and she and Sarah were invited in. After introducing Sarah, Molly explained their interest.

Mr. Goski went into a back room and returned with a document of several pages. "Here's a list of the lawyers registered with The Association of the Bar of the City of New York. There's an Albert Gordon here and his office is at 17 Washington Street. That's near the Battery."

Molly wrote the address on a piece of paper. She thanked Mr. Goski profusely. The women hurried to the Western Union office several blocks away and sent their message to Albert Gordon. They were assured it would be delivered early the next day.

CHAPTER 13

▼

Albert Gordon was a partner in a small law firm specializing in immigration cases. His office was near the Battery in the southern section of New York City. Several of the federal courts were nearby. It was close to where Sarah and Molly had awaited the S. S. Netherlands.

It was Thursday, and Sarah and Molly had spent the day at work, much to the relief of their supervisor who had run out of patience about Sarah's absences. Sarah needed to keep her job and she didn't want to return to operating a sewing machine again. To show her value to the company, she worked especially hard that day and nearly caught up with the backlog of office tasks she had to perform.

The women showed up at Gordon's office soon after five thirty. They had come directly from work. As they opened the door, Albert stood up from his desk and moved toward them. Seeing Molly, he smiled and said "Molly. How nice to see you. I got your message early this afternoon."

He had first met Molly a couple of years earlier at his lecture about immigration law at the Young Men's Hebrew Association. Based on his talk and the short conversation they had afterward, she learned of his professional work and related to him some of her experiences as an immigrant. They had a couple of dates after that, but no serious relationship had developed.

"Albert, meet my friend, Sarah. We hope you can give us a few minutes for Sarah to tell you about a problem she has."

"I'm not a psychiatrist. I hope the problem's about immigration."

"Well, sort of."

Albert had the smaller of two rooms in an office on the fourth floor of an old building on Washington Street. The walls were bare, except for the filled bookcases and two framed documents behind his desk—one his law degree and the other his certificate of membership in the New York Bar.

It was his profound wish to become a judge some day. That wasn't out of the question yet, but it had been several years since he finished law school and he was still right where he started—in this law office. To eventually become a judge, you had to serve in a court in some capacity, preferably as a clerk to one of the sitting justices. Albert was capable of doing that, but he had no political connections. If you didn't know someone in Tammany Hall at that time who could give you a push in the right direction, it wasn't likely you would get a position in a court. And it wasn't to his advantage to be recognized as a Jew; anti semitism was widespread and Jews were excluded from areas of the workforce such as the justice system.

A dark green sofa sat in front of his desk, with wooden chairs on each side of it. A window provided a good view of that part of the city looking toward New York Harbor.

Albert invited the ladies to have seats. He began by asking Molly, "Do you still go to those lectures at the YMHA? I haven't seen you there lately."

Molly, pleased that he remembered where they had met, replied: "Oh, actually the two of us go there and also to Cooper Union whenever we can. Sarah has been in this country only two years. When I met you, Sarah and I didn't know each other yet."

Albert tried to put the women at ease. "Maybe I can join the two of you on one of your intellectual evenings out."

"We would like that, I'm sure," Molly said.

What Albert Gordon lacked in looks, he made up for with intelligence and charm. And how he loved to talk. Sarah saw right away that this short, dark haired man with a blotchy face and deep set brown eyes reminded her of some of the Jewish yeshiva students she knew in the old country. His large library indicated he was well read, especially in his law field. Sarah liked his nice manner. She felt at once he was the right person to look into this matter of the ship deaths. His degree and membership in the Bar meant he had the credentials.

"Well, what is the purpose of your visit today?" Albert inquired. "Sarah, tell me about your problem. Then I'll decide if I can help you."

As Sarah told her story, Albert took copious notes on a legal pad. She told of her meetings with, first, the Captain, and then the purser, and the later chance meeting with Lena Levin, who was a passenger on the ship. Sarah removed Julius's last letter to the family from her bag. She handed it to Albert.

"My brother was so excited to be joining us again, and my family was anxiously waiting for him." said Sarah.

After she concluded, Albert lowered his head a bit and said "I'm very sorry you lost your brother. I lost a sister in an accident a year ago and it was a very traumatic experience."

After a short pause, he went on, "Regarding your case, it's a very bizarre one indeed. Participants or witnesses in cases of this kind often give differing accounts of what happened but usually they aren't *so* different. The question is who was telling the truth, if any of them.

"Fortunately, you came at a good time." He glanced at Molly with a half smile. "My partner is out of town on a case and I just finished one." Looking at Sarah, he said, "What I can do for you, if you're interested, is to begin with investigation to see if there's any wrongdoing that makes for a legal case."

"What would that involve?" Sarah asked.

"Well, I would learn as much as I can about circumstances surrounding the different stories. I can talk with some people involved and I can find out what your brother and the other two left behind on the ship. I'd probably check information at the library and the newspaper office that could throw some light on the situation.

"But, first of all, if I'm going to take your case, I'll need your approval in writing for me to investigate and take necessary legal action. I have an agreement form that both of us would have to sign. It's our firm's practice." He pushed a piece of paper across the desk toward her. "That's an example. It's protection for both the client and the lawyer."

Sarah interrupted him. "First, I need to know how much this will cost. I talked with my father and he has some money to pay you for this, but not a lot."

Albert laughed, then apologized for his laughter, and said he understood but not to worry. "Lawyers have a way of figuring out who can pay and who can't, and our firm charges accordingly. From what you've told me, this case sounds quite fascinating. With your consent, I'll proceed.

"We must move quickly on this case if we're able to come to some conclusion about who was at fault and take proper action. I promise to be fair when I tell you we will negotiate the fee at the close."

Sarah was a bit uneasy about such an uncertain proposal, but she wanted to trust him. She glanced in Molly's direction and got a nod. Albert then filled out part of the consent form and signed his name to it. Sarah read it over and signed it "Sarah Newman, on behalf of the Nathan Newman family" and gave her address.

Albert asked Sarah some questions about her discussions with the various people, and added her answers to his notes.

"Don't you have someone to help you on this?" Sarah asked.

"This is a small firm. Just my partner and me. We hire temporary help when there's lots to do. I believe I can handle this one myself. If I decide along the way I need help, I'll hire someone.

"First," he said, "I'll go to the court and ask for an injunction to prevent anyone involved in the case from leaving the city. That would give me time to investigate and, if necessary, present findings to an immigration hearing judge for possible action. I can do that in the morning.

"Second, I'll go to the Astor Library to read about cholera, and to the New York Times to find out what areas of Europe have recently been affected by the disease.

"Third, I'll get permission to enter the immigration station at Ellis Island and examine the belongings your brother and the other two had been carrying on the ship. I know that such material is kept in a locked room at the arrival location for safekeeping, even for those who die on board. What is and isn't in the baggage might provide some clues.

"Fourth, I'll meet with Mrs. Levin to ask her some questions. Perhaps she knows more; perhaps she knows less."

"Finally, after I have done my investigation, and assuming I have sufficient information, we'll ask for a court hearing. The outcome of the hearing will determine if any legal action is warranted."

Sarah agreed with Albert's plan. He told Sarah to contact him in a few days if he hadn't already gotten in touch with her.

He also noted where Lena was staying and where Sarah could be reached at work. "I will contact you as soon as I can if I have something to report.

"Another thing, if you get any new information, write it down on a sheet of paper and slip it under my office door.

Sarah said that she would. "Is there anything else I can do now?"

"Nothing at the moment," Albert told her. "You need to be present if and when we go before a judge. We might need to have Mrs. Goetz here as well, but I don't have to decide that now"

The women left Albert busily writing more notes.

When Albert was through writing, he checked his address book and found the name of a lawyer friend, Jim Davis, who was a clerk for Judge Addison Brown at the federal Southern District Court of New York City. That was where most of the immigration cases were handled.

Packing his briefcase with some papers and his notes, he dashed over to the nearby courthouse. Although it was past seven o'clock, Davis was still there and helped Albert file a request for an injunction to prevent the principal persons the case from leaving the New York area, at least until after a hearing on the case was completed. It was to be delivered Friday morning to Judge Brown.

CHAPTER 14

▼

Albert Gordon often wondered why he became an immigration lawyer. He had been born in New York City and lived all his life there. While he was growing up, he often saw people who had recently come to this country and he felt compassion for them and the difficulties they frequently faced. That probably had something to do with the legal specialty he chose.

But there was something else. He recalled that, when he was a child, his father spoke to him one day about how he and his wife came to the United States.

"Your mother and I were both German Jews. I was born in Frankfurt and your mother in Aachen. We didn't know each other, nor did our families ever meet. In fact, when I was seven, my parents moved to England and changed their name from Groen to Gordon. My father had been in business and he thought both going to another country and taking a new name would give him a fresh start.

"It didn't work out that way. So, when I was about ten we followed some relatives to this country. Life for us has been good ever since.

"Meanwhile, your mother remained in Germany until she was six. Her family joined two sets of neighbors and emigrated to America. They settled in the section of New York around 61st and 62nd Streets. There was a concentration of German Jews in that area. My family lived a couple of blocks away. Your mother and I met in the public school, became good friends, and eventually married. And you, our first child, became our greatest accomplishment."

His father's story always stuck in his mind. When he was in law school, he became interested in laws affecting immigrants and he suspected his father's account of his parents coming to America had something to do with it.

Albert was a conscientious fellow; yet, even he wondered if he could accomplish all the tasks he outlined to Sarah in a short period of time. He thought about hiring a clerk but decided it would take longer to get one and explain what he wanted him to do than to do it himself. He had no time to waste. He would do as much as he could on Friday and finish his investigation on Monday.

Albert hopped into a horse drawn coach and directed the driver to 425 Lafayette Street, where the Astor Library was located. He had done research there before. It was the largest reference library in the New York area and not far from his office.

Arriving there, he marveled at the stately structure and found even more wondrous the collection of informational sources the Library contained. In his earlier visits there, he discovered records of all types, from census reports to writings of ancient prophets and more contemporary literary masterpieces.

Albert obtained his entrance card, a requirement of the Library to keep track of their users and legitimate their purposes of studying there. He made his way to the main research room. That was where he knew he could be directed to information on medical history.

To expedite matters, he unhesitatingly approached the desk and asked one of the librarians: "Can you help me find some information concerning the history of cholera?"

After asking Albert whether he was interested in a particular country or anywhere in the world and getting his reply, the librarian disappeared for at least fifteen minutes before returning with several publications, including a volume of an encyclopedia. He thanked her, found space at a study table, and started flipping through the book indexes.

He first spotted an explanation of cholera in the encyclopedia and copied two passages into his notebook.

It is an intestinal infection caused by contaminated water and food. It could last up to five days and those infected can experience severe dehydration and vomiting and death if treatment cannot be provided. It is seldom passed along from direct person to person contact and is more common among children than adults....

The disease was first identified in India in 1826 and caused the deaths of untold numbers, and was carried by soldiers to various parts of Europe. Cholera epidemics appeared in many countries of Europe throughout the 1800's. Its most devastating effects were in Central and Eastern Europe. In 1873, a couple of hundred thousand persons died of it in Germany and Hungary.

Albert checked the other references but found nothing beyond similar definitions. He returned the books to the cart for books to be reshelved and thanked the librarian who had helped him.

Quickly exiting the building, he walked sprightly the several blocks to Park Row, where the New York Times offices were located. The Times was the leading newspaper of the New York area and included on its masthead the phrase "All the news that's fit to print." Albert wasn't so sure about that, but he agreed it was the best paper in town and did have good coverage of most newsworthy topics.

In the lobby of the building, he approached a gentleman at a desk and asked where he could find information on recent outbreaks of cholera. The man, a receptionist and not especially knowledgeable about detailed contents of past papers, told him, "Go upstairs one flight and turn left. Our researchers are in the second room on the right. They can help you."

He followed instructions, got to the room, and introduced himself to a young lady near the door. He repeated his request. She led him to an area where back issues of the newspaper were filed and showed him where he could sit to read them. Several people sat at other tables in the room, each poring over a single issue of the Times.

Albert scooped up as many of the most recent back issues of the paper he could carry to his table. Starting with the most recent issue, he thumbed through the papers and cast his eyes on headlines that referred to disease reports. After a while, he found he could expedite his search by restricting his examination to a few sections of the papers.

The twenty sixth paper he examined provided what he was looking for. There was an article on the first page about a cholera outbreak in Europe.

After a general discussion of the disease and its impact on immigrants, a sentence in the article read:

The most recent outbreak was in Hamburg in January of 1892.

He found nothing in the article to indicate the disease being prevalent at any time in Rotterdam or Boulogne. Then again, the encyclopedia article suggested a lag time and a five day spell of the disease.

From his reading, Albert concluded that it was possible that Abe, Rivka, and Julius had carried the disease from other places to the ship and that its effect was only realized after the ship was at sea for a few days. However, it was unlikely that three persons traveling some distance before boarding the ship, through different places and two of them boarding at different cities, could have acquired the disease without others on the ship also having experienced it. Thus, the Captain's story was possible but not probable.

Albert stuffed his notes into his briefcase and left the building. He took a few deep breaths of the outside air and walked hurriedly to the southern tip of Manhattan Island. It was an overcast day but no rain was forecast, and the walk would do him good after sitting so much. He took in the sights along the way and enjoyed observing activities on the streets. He passed Chinatown and noted the rows of eateries and laundries, the names of the establishments in Chinese letters above the doors or on the windows. Several peddlers approached him to offer him "something special," but he waved them off. In the alleyways on a few streets, he saw a few "down and outers" sleeping on makeshift pallets with their ragged belongings alongside.

At last, he arrived at the pier. A ferryboat headed for Ellis Island had just departed and had begun crossing the Harbor. A number of people were already in line for the next one. A dispatcher called out, "Stay in your line. The next ferry will arrive shortly and will leave for Ellis Island in about twenty minutes."

Albert quipped to himself, "If only I had walked more quickly or taken a buggy ride, I might have made that last ferry. Well, that's life." A concession stand was offering food and drinks. It was lunchtime now and Albert, after asking the person behind him in line to save his place, bought a sandwich and a cream soda and consumed them while he waited.

The next ferry had arrived and the gates were opened for travelers. Albert went aboard and moved to the far end where there was an open area that was a good observation point. Leaning against the ferry rail, he looked up at the gigantic Statue of Liberty in the harbor across from Ellis Island and tipped his hat as if to say, "You keep watch and I'll figure this one out."

. When the ferry docked at Ellis Island, he went to the records office. From his work, he knew many of the personnel who staffed Ellis Island's immigrant station. After identifying himself as a member of the Bar, he asked to see the manifest of the S. S. Netherlands on its most recent voyage. The clerk, who was a new one, asked for the date of arrival. "This past Tuesday, May 23," said Albert, a bit irritated that someone should be testing him. Some minutes passed before the clerk returned with the manifest and handed it to Albert, after getting him to sign his name on the borrower's sheet.

Albert carried it over to a small table and scanned the pages. He identified the names of the three deceased persons, listed in sequence.

Newman, Julius Benjamin 24 Pharmacist
Borchowitz, Rivka 38 Seamstress
Solomon, Abraham 45 Tailor

The information was entered at the ports of embarkation. Someone, presumably the purser, had crossed through the names with a thin stroke of a pen and had written "Deceased" at the end of each line.

Albert made notes of the entries and returned the manifest to the clerk with half hearted thanks. He then quickly made his way to the storage area where arrivals were required to leave their baggage until their examinations were complete. Only after immigrants had passed the inspections were they allowed to recover their belongings and board the ferries for the city.

He greeted a guard with whom he was familiar. "Hey, Jim, still at the old post, I see."

"Another tough case?" Jim asked.

"Maybe tough, maybe not so tough," answered Albert.

Albert knew the purser would have deposited the baggage in the storage area.

"Look, Jim, I need to find the baggage of three passengers on the S. S. Netherlands who died at sea. How about letting me in the storage room?"

"If it's really important to you, I can do it."

Albert slipped some coins into Jim's pocket.

"Much obliged," said the guard.

It took a while before Albert located the tagged baggage he was looking for. The items in the room were stacked on top of each other and he had to move a lot of them to the side before he found the right ones. When he realized that the bags he wanted had green tags on them whereas the majority had red or yellow tags, it made the task easier.

He pulled the bags with green tags next to a small table. Raising one marked with Julius Benjamin Newman's name, he opened it. It was a small bag containing some common medicinal items. Albert looked through the contents carefully, examining each item. He then smelled the bag for unusual odors. "*Nothing out of the ordinary,*" he mumbled to himself.

He then turned to a second, much larger bag, also with Newman's name on it. This one included some clothes and a number of personal items. He looked at the label on one of the jackets and read that it was made in Warsaw. He was interested in one pair of trousers that had fashionable stripes of brown and tan. "Haven't seen anything like this in New York," he thought to himself. Digging deeper in the bag, he came across a couple of letters from a young woman with a Polish surname. The letters had been mailed from New York.

Albert opened one of them:

Life in America is all I expected it would be. It seems so long since we last saw each other in Warsaw. I treasure your loving letters. My heart is aching for you, my dear Julius, and I don't know if I can wait until you arrive. My new address is 379 West 13th Street, Apt. 17. I will welcome you here with Love,

Your Etta

Albert opened the other letter to Julius, also from Etta, which contained similar sentiments. He wondered how long since this romance had begun and what Julius had said in his letters to her.

He added this evidence to what he had already learned about Julius from his sister. He thought it unlikely that Julius would have become enamored of a woman like Rivka, one much older than he. He didn't know how old Etta was, but she expressed herself as a younger woman would.

The letters from Etta, as well as the letter his sister had received from him before he left for Boulogne, didn't give any indication that Julius was upset or distraught. Moreover, nothing in his baggage or knowledge of his background would have predicted any criminal behavior.

He closed the bag. On the face of it, the purser's contention that Newman had poisoned Solomon, and inadvertently Borchowitz, and then took poison himself seemed far fetched. The evidence wasn't sufficient to establish his innocence but it certainly wasn't damning.

Albert scribbled notes on the pad he brought with him. He then examined the tags of the other luggage and lifted one marked "Abraham Solomon" to the table.

It was a heavy bag. He opened it and discovered a Hebrew Torah, a prayer shawl, a *mezuzah*, some small books, a few family documents, and several pieces of clothing, including a partially sewn pair of suit pants and a hand sewn jacket.

The copy of the Torah had an inscription inside the front cover. It was written in Yiddish. Albert struggled to read it and finally concluded it was in the hand of Abe's *zayde*, his grandfather, given on the occasion of Abe's *bar mitzvah.* Albert snickered. He, himself, had such a gift inscribed by his father in safekeeping.

Notes written in Yiddish on the back of a marriage record listed what seemed to Albert were the names of Abe's parents and his brothers and sisters. Albert studied them and wondered where the rest of the family was located.

He examined the suit. It was finely sewn but unfinished. Knowing Abe had been a tailor, he imagined the conscientious way Abe had been fashioning the clothing. Albert shook his head. "What a beautiful piece of work," he murmured. He fingered the cloth and ran his hand over the jacket sleeves and pockets.

He put away Abe's bag. There were two bags left, with Rivka Borchowitz's name on both. Albert decided to open the suitcase. There were some letters, various pieces of clothing, and a few small personal items, including some inexpensive jewelry. He looked at a couple of the letters, presumably from family members and friends, which his limited reading of Yiddish suggested expressions of good wishes and warnings about being careful while traveling. Nothing in the suitcase seemed out of the ordinary.

A large cloth bag had a double knot in the rope that secured it. It took Albert several minutes to untie it. Opening it wide, he saw only a few photographs and some letters, the whole of which hardly filled the bag. The photos were tintypes and considerably faded; he could make out the faces of some of the people he assumed were family members.

If, as he was told, the bag had once carried silver items, and especially a candelabra, they were now in the possession of someone else. There was room for such objects but no evidence of them.

Sheyna Goetz had told Sarah it was common practice for women to bring with them at least a few pieces of family silver from the old country. Sarah had mentioned to Albert that Lena claimed she remembered that Rivka was carrying silver pieces in her bag. If that was true, it was apparent that such items had been stolen. To confirm that, Albert would have to talk to some of the other women who had been steerage passengers on the S. S. Netherlands to ask if they had been shown the candelabra or other silver items during the early part of the voyage. But, except for Mrs. Levin, finding these other women would be difficult and time consuming.

Albert called Jim over and told him he was finished with his examination of the bags, but that they may have to be used in a court hearing. It would be best, he said, to keep them separated from the rest.

It was late afternoon that Friday when Albert finished his work at Ellis Island and caught the ferry back. He believed he had time to stop at the Courthouse before going to Mrs. Cohen's to talk with her sister.

Hurrying to Pearl Street, he found Jim Davis still at the Courthouse and discussed with him the urgency of a hearing as early the following week as possible. Time was crucial and waiting beyond Monday might create problems because of the S. S. Netherlands' scheduled return to Rotterdam. The ship line would object to the Court extending the injunction so long that it delayed the departure unreasonably.

Albert felt he could arrange his notes adequately to make a presentation and ask questions of witnesses by the beginning of the week. Davis explained how getting the injunction was simple compared to getting a place on the Court docket. "There is already a backlog of cases. Some additional judges are being brought in to hear cases, but the schedules aren't set yet. Let's wait until Monday morning and I'll present your arguments for the expedited process. I usually meet for a half hour with Judge Brown first thing on Mondays." Albert thanked him and said he would pass along the status of court matters to the ship line.

Albert, satisfied with the promise, headed for Mrs. Cohen's.

When he arrived at the address given to him by Sarah, he knocked on the door and Mrs. Cohen opened it. Sarah had told her that "Mr. Albert," a lawyer who was helping her, might be visiting that day.

Albert exchanged pleasantries with Mrs. Cohen and apologized for the late hour before Max and Lena Levin came into the room. Although they knew what Sarah had told Mrs. Cohen, they were suspicious of Albert's purpose. "Lawyers and investigators in the old country were up to no good," Max had observed wryly.

He and Lena were persuaded by Mrs. Cohen to cooperate and answer Albert's questions. "Mr. Gordon is not a government investigator," said

Mrs. Cohen, who served tea to her guest. "You can trust him. He is help-ing Sarah find out what really happened on the ship."

"What's to find?" said Lena. "I already told Sarah what I know."

Albert thanked both Lena and Max for agreeing to talk with him. He then asked Lena, with Mrs. Cohen translating, to repeat for him what she saw or heard on the ship relating to the deaths.

"Sarah told me your story, but I have to have it in writing for my inves-tigation. I must hear it from you myself."

Lena looked at Max, heaved a big sigh, and started to tell Albert her story. The tale was essentially the same as what Sarah had reported. How-ever, some of the details were different—who she heard the rumor from, when she heard it, and where she was at the time.

Several times while she was giving her story, Max interrupted her to suggest variations in reported facts. Albert discouraged him, unless he had firsthand knowledge of the incident. Lena finished her story and added: "Beasts. They were beasts."

Albert noted the apparent discrepancies in Lena's story, but he also noted that it had been almost two weeks since the event took place. Often, memories fade with time. Lena's story seemed plausible. Even if it was true, what remained undetermined was whether the thieves were sailors on the ship or other passengers.

Albert was also bothered about Lena's emphasis on the treatment of women by the sailors. He had wanted to ask her if she had been bothered personally by members of the crew; however, he didn't feel comfortable asking that question. So he asked Mrs. Cohen to put the question in her own words to Lena, whose translated reply was "They touched me. That's all I want to say."

It was now nearly seven o'clock. Thanking Mrs. Cohen for her hospital-ity and the Levins for their assistance, Albert excused himself. Sarah lived close by, and he went to her apartment to tell her what had transpired dur-ing the day.

"I've covered a lot of ground today," he told her when she met him at the door.

Sarah introduced him to her mourning parents and sister Feyga, who were sitting *shiva* in remembrance of their son and brother.

Mr. Newman thanked Albert for his help. He said he regretted not having come to his office. "I asked Sarah to see you because she knew so much about details," he said. "We're still in shock, as you can imagine, but our family wants to find out what really happened to Julius. We can't accept that he was responsible for any deaths. Not our Julius."

"I understand," said Albert. He asked if they would like him to report to them what he'd found out that day.

"Please, please," Mr. Newman encouraged him.

Albert related to them his discoveries at the library, the Times, and Ellis Island and his talk with Mrs. Cohen's sister. He mentioned that court papers would be served on them to appear before the Court sometime early in the week.

"I can imagine how you must be feeling. I hope we can understand the situation better after the court hearing. *Gut shabbes.*" He departed for his apartment with the intention of starting preparations for the hearing but he knew he would not get very far with it that night.

CHAPTER 15

▼

When he awoke Saturday morning, Albert was feeling the stiffness in his legs from all the walking he had done the day before. Daylight was peeking through the curtains. He couldn't believe he had gotten a full night's sleep.

He first thought he might go to see Sarah, but then he realized it was time for synagogue services. Being only a "holiday" Jew, he wouldn't be attending. Sarah's father and others in the family would be going, especially to say prayers for Julius. Unless he was to join them, it was better for him not to be seen there.

He dressed, had a bit of breakfast, and then retrieved his notes on the case. Reading through them, he struggled to come up with the true scenario of what had happened on the ship. The fact he hadn't personally spoken with the Captain or the Purser struck him as a gap in his investigation. "Not that Sarah's account of what the two had told her is erroneous in any way," he mused. "It would strengthen my information if I could talk with them and maybe add a few insights that didn't come out of the meetings with Sarah."

If he got to the Captain's hotel before noon, he might catch him before he strolled somewhere in the city. He checked his notes and saw that the Captain was staying at the Hotel Esplanade on 24th Street near Eighth Avenue. That was just a few blocks from his bachelor apartment on West 21st Street. He could get there in about fifteen minutes. Grabbing a small notebook and a couple of pencils, and after massaging his stiff legs, he headed out the door for the hotel.

It was warming up outside and the air smelled fresh after a brief shower during the night. He had no trouble finding the hotel. The front of it was just as Sarah had described. He stopped a moment before going in to review in his mind what he wanted to say to the Captain.

The desk clerk greeted him and asked if he wanted a room. "No, but I am here to visit someone," replied Albert. "Mr. Meergossen."

"Oh, the Captain," the clerk responded. "Is he expecting you?"

"No, but it's on an important matter. Do you know if he is in?"

"I haven't seen him leave this morning. Take the elevator to the second floor. He's in 214."

Albert thanked the clerk and followed his instructions. He had to knock twice before the door was opened. Before him stood the Captain, just how Sarah described him but now wearing a light sweater and gray pants instead of his ship uniform.

Not recognizing Albert, the Captain was at first hesitant to invite him into the room. "I am a friend of Sarah's and would like to talk with you about the unfortunate deaths at sea," explained Albert, after introducing himself. The Captain then ushered him into the room and offered him a chair.

"What can I do for you?" asked the Captain.

"I am trying to help the family cope with the terrible loss of their son and brother. The best way for me to do that is to try to confirm what happened on the ship and then get the family to accept that information as final. They are still in shock and need of some assistance from others."

"I understand," said the Captain. "I told Miss Newman everything I know. The nurse's report of cholera was based on her training and knowledge. And putting the bodies of the three people into the sea is what we are required to do when passengers die and we are more than a couple of days from a port."

"Yes," said Albert. "But there are a couple of details I would like to explore further. I understand you told Sarah that cholera was common on shipboard these days and that no one else on the ship but the three were diagnosed with it. Is that correct?"

"Yes, that is correct."

"I am told there haven't been any cases of cholera reported on ships coming to America for a year now."

"There has been less of it this past year, but outbreaks of cholera take place from time to time. And it has been reported recently on ships going to other places in the world. You see, there is no fixed pattern to it. It can turn up almost anywhere at almost anytime. Unfortunately, it was found on my ship during this last voyage."

"And the fact that only these three people acquired it, and no one else on the ship. Isn't that peculiar?"

"It *is* peculiar, certainly. I don't know what to make of it. One can speculate about several ways it could have come about. I spoke to Miss Newman about that as well."

"Were there any other deaths on the ship other than of those three?"

"No, and we carry many passengers; it was at least three hundred on this trip."

"Then there is no doubt in your mind that the three who died on the ship were victims of cholera, and we can close the record on this incident?"

"Exactly, exactly."

Albert thought for a moment and then inquired of the Captain, "Have you been in touch with the purser since you came to this hotel?"

"No, he is staying with friends and we will meet at the ship when it is time to return to Holland."

"Did you receive papers from the Court here in New York stating that you and other members of your ship's staff should not leave the New York area until given permission?"

"Yes, those papers were delivered to me. We get such papers every once in a while when there is some question about the ship. It probably will delay our return, but that is not my business. The owners of the ship have to deal with that."

Albert didn't believe any further questions of the Captain would be productive, except one. "Have you heard any more from your ship's nurse?"

"She is traveling in the country. I told Miss Newman that the nurse would not be returning with us, so what she is doing now is of little consequence for me."

"Thank you for your courtesy," said Albert, shaking hands with the Captain. "I hope you can make your return voyage before too long."

When he got back to the street, Albert decided to pay a visit to the Purser. If the Captain's story could not be shaken, maybe the Purser's can. Looking at his notes about the Purser, he found the address—903 West 51st Street. He was staying with a family named Naflick. Albert was still in a walking mood, so he headed directly north. When he reached 42nd Street, he realized it was lunchtime. He stopped at a cart to buy a potato knish and ate it as he continued toward the designated address.

At the apartment building he was looking for, he entered the small vestibule and spotted the Naflick name on the mailbox for apartment 10. The apartments on the first floor were numbered 1 through 5. He climbed the stairs and found number 10 at the end of the hall. He rapped on the door. Getting no reply, he rapped again; then, a third time.

Exiting the building, he crossed the street to a city park and sat on a bench that faced the apartment building. He could see who came and went, and the description of LaFontaine given by Sarah would help spot him. If he saw others come or go he would approach them to ask about the purser.

Roughly an hour passed and no one was seen entering or exiting the building. Albert returned to the Naflick apartment and rapped on the door several times. Maybe someone had been sleeping there and didn't hear his earlier knocks. But there wasn't any response now, either.

"The occupants could be anywhere," he thought. "I'll come back tomorrow."

Albert spent the rest of Saturday at home working on his stamp collection, the only real hobby he had. Obtaining the stamps was a challenge.

Discovering the history behind the pictures on the stamps was what really attracted him. He learned a lot of history that way.

On Sunday morning, he bought the New York Times and read it from the first page to the last. He was interested in all sorts of news reports, and he also thought he might chance upon an article about cholera. There was lots of news in the paper but nothing about cholera.

After dressing appropriately for the outdoors, he made his way to the Naflick apartment on 51st Street. He knocked lightly on the door, then a bit harder. The door to the next apartment opened and a man stuck out his head and said, "I believe they're gone for the weekend but I don't know where."

Albert was miffed. "The Purser is in violation of the Court injunction if he's left the New York area," he mumbled. "I can understand if LaFontaine wants to see the sights. Being in New York and remaining in your apartment would not be entertaining. I just hope he'll be available when the hearing takes place."

In need of relaxation, Albert hopped on a buggy and asked the driver to take him to Central Park. He was always amazed by the Park. As the development of the city pushed northward, here in the middle of Manhattan Island a huge piece of land was dedicated to preservation of nature. It initially ran from 59th Street to 106th Street between Fifth and Eighth Avenues. There were no houses, apartment buildings, or office buildings on the land.

Albert had read that the idea for the Park began in 1844 with the suggestion coming from a newspaper editor named William Cullen Bryant. Somehow, the local political parties agreed to pay more than five million dollars for the vast undeveloped land. In 1857 Frederick Law Olmsted, the designated superintendent of the Park, and a lawyer named Calvert Vaux produced the design for the Park's layout based on their familiarity with the celebrated parks in European cities. One of the Park's commissioners, Andrew Haswell Green, steered the plan to its completion and also convinced city officials to extend the boundaries of the Park to 110th Street.

Albert delighted in strolling through vast sections of the area. He was particularly enamored of the lake created in the midst of the Park. It had been stocked with a large number of white swans, a beauty to behold. Some distance from the lake, across gently rolling hills, was an animal menagerie featuring a couple of young black bears.

Albert inhaled the beautiful environment of the Park. It was a fitting capstone to his Sunday outing and quieted his nerves.

Late Monday morning, Albert checked into his office. The cleaning woman had been there earlier and had spruced up the office a bit. It was still dingy and badly in need of decoration. He emptied his briefcase and pulled together his various notes on the case. He studied them once more.

It was time to nail down the date and time for the hearing. Albert walked to the Court. He found Jim Davis, conscientious person that he was, working busily at his desk.

Seeing Albert approaching, Jim looked up and said, "I have good news for you. I met with Judge Brown this morning and made your argument. He was sympathetic but at first wasn't sure how he could squeeze the case into his schedule.

"You know, Judge Brown is the sole judge at the Court and a specialist in admiralty law. He was intrigued when I explained the case to him. He told me he had a full load of cases to deal with himself for the week but he had invited two judges from neighboring areas to assist him in reducing the case load. One of them, Judge Raymond Smith, is from New Jersey and has promised to spend the week here to move cases along. Judge Brown asked him to take on this case and expedite it. He recognized that the ship line will be in a bind if their schedule of cross Atlantic voyages gets inordinately delayed. He suggested holding the hearing on Wednesday at one o'clock. He said that would give enough time for Judge Smith to familiarize himself with the facts and the issues and for witnesses to be notified and ready to be at the Court."

Judge Smith, after consenting to hold a hearing on Wednesday, had asked Jim to quickly dispatch messengers to the people Albert wanted present at the hearing and serve them with a notice to appear in court by one o'clock sharp on Wednesday. The hearing would determine whether a trial was justified.

Albert thanked Jim for arranging the hearing.

"Quite all right," replied Jim. "Remember that you now owe me a favor. *I* won't forget."

They shook hands and Albert departed, a smile on his face.

Sarah and Molly were busy at their jobs at Manhattan Needleworks. Mr. Greenstein was grateful for Sarah's return and inquired about the investigation and when "all that business" will be finished.

Sarah felt a little jumpy about his inquiry, knowing full well that Albert was trying to arrange a court hearing that could extend matters.

She went home during the lunch period to check on her mother. Her father and Feyga were back at work, and her mother was home alone. She knew Momma would still be depressed and a brief visit might be helpful.

Her mother was pleased to see her and told her that a messenger had come to the door only a half hour ago with a letter from the court for Sarah. "It's over on the table," she said. Sarah opened the envelope and read it:

"Judge Raymond Smith, on behalf of the U.S. District Court for the Southern District of New York, will be conducting a hearing on the case of three passengers on the S. S. Netherlands who died at sea in May 1893.

Proceedings will begin at one o'clock on Wednesday, May 31 in the Court's Chambers at 500 Pearl Street.

Your attendance is required."

The order was signed by James Davis, Clerk of the Court.

During their afternoon break, Sarah and Molly slid over to a corner of the room for a confidential conversation. Sarah showed Molly the court order. "My attendance is required. I doubt the hearing will go past Wednesday, but I need to show this to Mr. Greenstein. He won't be happy about it but it's a government requirement."

Sarah decided to wait until the workday was ended. For the rest of the afternoon she had difficulty keeping her mind on her duties. When the bell rang that signified time to stop work and go home, Sarah approached Mr. Greenstein and showed him the order. He read it and contorted his face. "I guess there isn't anything I can do about it if the government says so. I'll have to speak to the owner and tell him how your absences have affected our business. I'll see what he says."

In other parts of the city, the court order was delivered to people Albert had wanted to examine at the hearing. His plan for the case seemed to moving on schedule.

On Tuesday, Albert got to his office to find that his partner Fred Jacobs had returned, his out of-town business completed.

"Anything new?" Fred asked.

"Yes, and I've worked real hard since late Thursday." He elaborated his new case. "It's one of a kind. Three immigrant passengers die on a ship in a mysterious way. We have no available eyewitnesses to the deaths. Three different explanations have been given on how they died—the Captain's, the Purser's, and a woman passenger's. The ship's nurse, who examined the decedents, cannot be located. We're talking about people who never even arrived in the U.S. Their bodies were dropped into the ocean. The case is complicated. Maybe there's not a definite explanation. I gathered a lot of information on Friday and Saturday. The family of one of the deceased is determined to find out what happened, and it's them I'm working for."

"What's next?" Fred asked.

"A hearing is set for one tomorrow afternoon at the District Court before Judge Raymond Smith. He's helping Judge Brown with his case load. I got an injunction from the Court to keep potential witnesses in the New York area until the hearing is over and maybe after that. They've now gotten court orders to appear for the hearing tomorrow afternoon."

"You've been a busy person," Fred said, and he strolled into his office.

Albert emptied his briefcase and sorted through his drafts of statements he would make to the Court. He spent the rest of the morning reviewing and refining them. Every once in a while, he would jump up, go to Fred's office, and ask him, "What do you think about this?" Fred was older and more experienced and often made good suggestions.

At noon he and Fred walked across the street to a popular lunch place. They found a small table in the corner that suited them fine and ordered soup and crackers.

Albert asked, "How many times have you appeared before Judge Smith?"

"Twice, I believe. He visits here every once in a while."

"This will be my first. I was scheduled to appear before him once before but the case was dismissed. Is he fair?"

"Seemed fair to me. You know, every case has its peculiarities and a judge might see some things in a different way than you do."

After lunch, they walked over to the Harbor and watched tugboats pulling loads southward, probably heading around the bend to the eastside piers. Albert and Fred chatted along the way about each of their cases.

As the day was coming to a close, Albert decided he wanted to see Sarah and talk with her about the case. He loaded up his briefcase and made his way to her family's apartment. Mr. Newman had arrived a short while before and answered the door.

"Hello, Mr. Newman. Is Sarah home yet?"

"Hello, Albert. She and I got home the same time but she went over to Molly's. I don't know how long she'll be there."

"Are you and Mrs. Newman all right?"

"As well as can be expected. My wife tells me Sarah got a notice about a court hearing tomorrow afternoon. I'll ask my boss to let me take the afternoon off so Sadie and I can be there."

"Wonderful. I hope we can clear everything up at the hearing. I think I'll go over to Molly's to see Sarah. And I'll see you and your wife tomorrow."

Outside, children were playing hopscotch and ring around the rosy. Albert had to tiptoe to avoid interfering with the games. He crossed the street and walked toward Molly's apartment. As he neared it, he could see Sarah and Molly sitting on the stoop in front of Molly's building. They spotted him as well and waved for him to join them. He took a seat next to them on the stoop.

Turning toward Sarah, he said, "I hear you got your court order. I hope everyone else who's supposed to be there got one too."

"Are you ready for the hearing?" asked Molly.

"Probably as ready as I'll ever be. One thing bothers me. Saturday I went to visit the Captain. I wanted to see if he changed his story at all. He didn't. Seemed to be a nice man. Then I went to the place where you saw the Purser, Sarah, and no one was there. I hung around for a while with no luck. Even went back the next morning. A neighbor told me the people there had gone on a trip. I hope the purser didn't violate the injunction and go out of town. More importantly, I hope he shows up tomorrow."

"When I told my supervisor about taking off tomorrow afternoon," said Sarah, "he wasn't very happy—said he was going to talk with the owner. I sure am counting on the hearing finishing tomorrow. If not, I might have to look for a new job."

Molly spoke up. "That wouldn't be right."

"I agree," said Albert, "but life isn't always fair. Let's wait and hope for the best."

"I'll have to work all day tomorrow," said Molly. "Gee, I wish I could be at the hearing. As soon as my work finishes in the afternoon, I'll rush over to the Court. Maybe it won't be over yet and I can hear the decision of the Judge."

The three of them got up and, at Molly's invitation, went up to her apartment so she could introduce Albert to her family. The sun was falling behind the buildings across the street. When it arose again, Albert would be getting ready to find out how well his legal skills would be received in the Circuit Court.

CHAPTER 16

▼

Albert awoke on Wednesday full of excitement. "Maybe nothing will come of all this," he thought to himself, "but I'll probably never have another case as interesting and challenging as this one."

He considered going to the Naflick apartment once more to track down LaFontaine and get a statement from him before the court hearing. He weighed the pros and cons and reasoned it might be helpful if he found him but unproductive and consuming of valuable time if he didn't. Time was now of the essence, so he dismissed it from his mind. He buckled down with his notes and drafted statement for the Court. He needed to make a good showing before Judge Smith.

He glanced at what he had written down about the interview with Mrs. Levin and thought: "What sticks in my mind is her repeated reference to "Beasts" in referring to members of the ship's crew. At least, that's how Mrs. Cohen translated what she was saying. I heard Mrs. Levin saying 'Behaimeh, behaimeh.' If I remember correctly, in Yiddish that can mean 'Beasts' but it more generally means 'animal' and in popular Yiddish a 'fool.' Did Mrs. Cohen translate accurately what Mrs. Levin was intending to say?"

He realized he was groping for meaningful interpretations of what his notes indicated. "The bigger issue," he told himself, "was who was telling the truth. That's what I have to determine."

He passed the rest of the morning alternately reading his material and going over to look out the window to see if the magnificent view would inspire him to break through the puzzle.

A little after twelve thirty, Albert packed his briefcase and left for the courthouse.

As he entered the Circuit Court chambers from the rear, he was astonished by the number of people already present. The hearing room was about thirty by fifty feet and filled with long tables and chairs instead of benches in front of a raised platform where the Judge would sit. The seats on each side of a middle aisle were nearly filled to capacity.

He looked around and saw Sarah and her family at one of the front tables. He presumed that the couple seated alongside them, talking to Sarah, were Sheyna Goetz and her husband. At the table just behind them were Lena and Max Levin and Mrs. Cohen. The Captain and another man he presumed was the purser were seated at the front table across the aisle, along with two representatives of the ship line.

"Well," Albert mumbled, "at least the Purser showed up this afternoon."

At the table behind them were six men he guessed were from the ship's crew. Albert had asked that some crew members be available as witnesses. He was told that the purser had identified these six as providing services to passengers in steerage. The ship's nurse had not yet been found. Most of the remaining seats were filled with court personnel and lawyers who would appear before Judge Smith at later times and wanted to see how he handled this case.

He ambled to the front of the room, placed his briefcase on the attorney's table, and then turned and spoke to those in the first two rows on Sarah's side. He greeted the Newmans and the Levins and introduced himself to Sheyna Goetz and her husband.

Returning to his table, Albert sat down and looked straight ahead, feeling very much alone.

He soon gave a sigh of relief when he was joined by Fred Jacobs. Albert quietly thanked him for coming.

Sarah stood up and took a couple of steps to where Albert was sitting. She whispered in his ear, "The Purser hasn't come."

Albert asked "Who is the man next to the Captain?"

"I believe he is one of the clerks I talked with at the ship line's office," she answered.

Albert turned around and surveyed the audience. He was dismayed by LaFontaine's absence. He commented to Fred about the situation.

Shortly after one o'clock, the District Court began its session. The Bailiff called the court to order and Judge Smith entered the room and took his seat at the bench. He wore a long black robe loosely tied in front but open enough that his business suit was apparent. He motioned to the Bailiff who announced to the audience, "Please be seated."

The Clerk of the Court made a statement:

"This is a preliminary hearing on factors related to the deaths at sea of Julius Benjamin Newman, Rivka Borchowitz, and Abraham Solomon, traveling on the S.S. Netherlands during the month of May 1893."

A few women in the audience cried softly.

Judge Smith offered the basis for the hearing:

"Because the bodies of the deceased cannot be recovered, and because the circumstances of their deaths were not officially explained on the ship's log, it is incumbent on the Court to hear this case and conclude what legal action, if any, is called for. We owe it to the families, who chose to come to America, to provide them with knowledge of the manner of their relatives' deaths and for their peace of mind.

"It is understood that this is a hearing, not a trial. The purpose of a hearing is to learn the facts of a case and to conclude who, if anyone, is culpable for any actions that are in violation of federal law as it is presently documented.

"The party petitioning for this hearing is the Nathan Newman family, whose son, Julius Benjamin Newman, was one of those who reportedly died aboard the S. S. Netherlands. However, the outcome of this hearing has bearing on legal actions related to the reported deaths of the other two persons, Abraham Solomon and Rivka Borchowitz, as well as Mr. Newman.

"Mr. Albert Gordon is counsel for the Nathan Newman family."

"Mr. Gordon, I understand you will summarize the reported facts of the case."

"Yes, Your Honor," said Albert, and he proceeded to present his legal brief. He explained that his brief was based on Sarah's reported experience at the Battery when she went to meet her brother on his arrival; her reported conversations with the Captain, the Purser, and Mrs. Levin; his own investigations; and his interviews of the Captain and Mrs. Levin.

Albert then read his statement. When he got to the part about Sarah's meeting with the Purser and reported their conversation, the Captain had a startled look on his face and then seemed to be in deep thought, but he said nothing.

Albert then asked the judge for permission to question Sarah, Mrs. Goetz, Mrs. Levin, the Captain, the Purser, and six crewmen.

Judge Smith granted the request and asked the Clerk of the Court to swear in Sarah Newman. She sat in the witness chair and tried to keep her poise. She was nervous and hoped no one noticed.

"You are Miss Sarah Newman. Is that correct?" asked Albert.

"Yes, correct."

"Are you related to any of the three people who died at sea?"

"Yes. Julius Newman is—was—my brother." At this point, Sarah lost her composure and dabbed her eyes with her handkerchief.

"Miss Newman, in my opening statement I summarized your reports of meetings with the Captain of the ship, the ship's purser, and Mrs. Levin. Was my account accurate?"

"Yes, it was."

"Did I leave out any significant facts that you can add now?"

"No. In each case, there was more conversation, but I believe you covered the important points."

"Miss Newman, was there anyone accompanying you when you met with the Captain at the hotel?"

"Yes, Mrs. Sheyna Goetz."

"Thank you, Miss Newman. You may step down now."

"Your Honor, I would like to question Mrs. Goetz next."

Sheyna Goetz was sworn in and went to the witness chair. She was biting her lips and smoothing her dress and looked to those she knew in the audience for support. After she seemed to be settled in her chair, she leaned over and picked up the pocketbook she had brought to the witness box. Rummaging through it, she pulled out a handkerchief which she kept in her hand.

"You are Mrs. Sheyna Goetz. Am I right?" asked Albert.

"Sheyna Goetz, yes. That's my husband sitting there at the front table."

"Thank you. From now on, please speak a little louder so everyone can hear you."

"I'm sorry. I'll do better."

"Mrs. Goetz, were you related to any of the people who died on the ship?"

"Two of them were cousins of mine—Abe Solomon and Rivka Borchowitz. I can't get over it. Why should such wonderful people die before they enjoy becoming Americans?"

"I sympathize with you, Mrs. Goetz. It shouldn't have happened. But our purpose now is to see if we can understand what caused their deaths. It seems that different explanations have been given by three people, and there can only be one truth."

"Go on with your case, Mr. Gordon" said Judge Smith.

Albert acknowledged the Judge's remark and continued his questioning of Mrs. Goetz.

"In my opening statement, I talked about you being with Miss Newman when she went to see the Captain. Were you with her, and was my summary of the visit accurate?"

"Yes, she came to my apartment to get me and we walked to the hotel together. And what was said in the Captain's hotel room—yes, that's the way I remember it. Sometimes my memory is not so good. But it only happened a few days ago and what you said is what was the discussion."

"So you have nothing important to add to what I said?

"Well, I guess everything can be important. The Captain told us what he knew about people on ships having cholera. You didn't mention that."

"Thank you for that addition, Mrs. Goetz.

"Am I right that you didn't go with Miss Newman to see the Purser?"

"No, I didn't go. I have two small children. Once in a while I can get someone to look after them. That's what I did when we went to see the Captain. The next day when Sarah visited the other man I had to stay home with the children."

"Thank you, Mrs. Goetz. You may return to your place next to your husband."

"Your Honor, my next witness will be Mrs. Lena Levin. Mrs. Levin has just come to this country and doesn't speak English yet. As I pointed out in my statement, she was a passenger on the ship in question. We have a person here in front of the bench to translate her testimony."

Lena was trembling as she rose from her seat in chambers, and Max embraced her to give her courage. She walked slowly toward the witness box, was sworn in with the help of the Yiddish translator, and took the stand.

She continued to be nervous and merely acknowledged that what she had told Sarah, reported by Albert in his initial summary, was essentially correct. She continued to speak. "It's terrible even to think about the tragedy, but at least now it's something I don't have to keep only in my mind."

"Mrs. Levin, do you recall that I spoke with you last Friday after you had already spoken with Miss Newman?"

"Of course. You came to my sister's apartment."

"Yes. What you told me then about what happened on the ship was similar to what you had told Sarah, but you seemed less sure about some things. I am thinking in particular about what you saw or heard yourself compared to what others told you they saw or heard."

"Well, sometimes it's hard to remember if what you know came from someone else or you learned it yourself. It's clear in my mind how this woman told several of us the story about Rivka. As for bodies being thrown overboard, I heard that myself, and others did too."

"Mrs. Levin, when you spoke to me about what took place on the ship you referred to the behavior of some members of the crew. Your sister, Mrs. Cohen, translated one of the words you used in speaking about those crew members as 'beasts.' The Yiddish word you spoke was, I believe, '*behaimeh*'. Did you mean 'beasts' or another meaning, which is 'fools'? There is an important difference there."

Lena bent over to have a conversation with the translator. After some discussion, she spoke again and the translator followed with "They were beasts, but they were also fools." Several people in the room giggled.

Albert asked her: "Can you identify any of the crew members in this courtroom as being on the ship?"

Lena looked slowly around the room and replied through the translator, "Mr. Gordon, I didn't see the killings myself, so I cannot identify any of the crew members involved."

"I am not asking about the deaths, Mrs. Levin. I am just asking if you recognize any crewmen from the ship in this courtroom."

Lena scanned the left side of the room. "That man over there (she pointed to one of them) looks like someone who bothered me on the ship. But I can't say for sure." There was more murmuring in the courtroom.

Albert resumed his questioning. "Will you tell the Court who the person or persons were who told you about members of the ship's crew killing the three people?"

Lena shook her head from side to side. Albert asked her to speak to the question. She answered "No, I don't remember her name."

Albert told the Judge he was through with this witness at this time but may want to call her back later. Judge Smith nodded his head.

The judge excused Lena, and Albert asked for the Captain as his next witness. The crowd had begun to shift around and talk among themselves. Judge Smith hit his gavel and asked for silence in the noisy courtroom.

Captain Meergossen was sworn in and asked to enter the witness box. He was sweating profusely, even though it was a relatively cool morning and fans were circulating the air in the courtroom.

Albert succinctly summarized the reported conversation between the Captain and Sarah and Sheyna. He then added from the notes he took when he met with the Captain himself. He turned to the Captain and asked: "Is that essentially what was said in your conversation with those ladies, and with me?"

The Captain said "Yes. That was the essence of our discussions."

"Are there any details I omitted that would be pertinent to this case?"

"M . m, I cannot think of any at the moment."

The door to the courtroom opened and a small, thin man entered. After looking around at who was there, he made his way to the table where the Captain had been sitting and occupied one of the empty chairs.

Sarah gave an "Ahem" to Albert, who turned around to see what she wanted. She pointed to the man who had just come in. Albert silently mouthed the word "Purser" and Sarah nodded her head.

Albert told the Judge he had no more questions for Captain Meergossen but would also want to be able to call him back to the stand. The Judge consented.

Albert then asked for permission to speak with the Judge. He went to the bench and told Judge Smith that he believed the man who had just entered the room was the Purser. The timing was right. He had expected to examine him next.

The Purser was called forward and sworn in. Once he was in the box, Judge Smith asked him what delayed his arrival.

"You must excuse me, Mr. Justice," he said. "The past few days have been difficult for me. My hostess here in New York and I were seeing the sights of the city when a misfortune occurred. She fell when going down some steps and it was necessary to take her to a hospital. The doctor said her leg was fractured and she needed to stay at the hospital for a few days. I remained close by to be of assistance to her until she could return to her dwelling. Because of the stressful situation, I did not return to her apartment until late this morning. That's when I discovered the message to report to this Court today. I came as quickly as I could."

Judge Smith asked Albert to go ahead with his questioning.

"Mr. LaFontaine," said Albert, "you were not here when I read a statement summarizing all of the relevant conversations concerning this case. Let me restate the portion that covers Miss Newman's meeting with you."

"Oh yes."

"When approached by Miss Newman about the deaths that occurred on the S. S. Netherlands during its recent voyage and what caused them, you are reported to have told her that a love triangle had developed with the three persons and that her brother, who was a pharmacist, put a deadly poison in a dessert given to Mr. Solomon, that Miss Borchowitz tasted that dessert, that both of them developed fatal symptoms and died soon after, and that her brother, heartbroken because a poison designed to kill Mr. Solomon had also killed Miss Borchowitz, soon after took his own life with the same poison. Is that what you told Miss Newman?"

"Yes, that is what I told her."

The Captain was shaking his head from side to side but made no comments.

Sadie Newman broke into tears. Her husband tried to comfort her.

"Mr. LaFontaine, that story of what happened is very disturbing. Has anything like that ever happened on one of your ship voyages before?"

"No, nothing exactly like that has happened on any of my other trips. But there have been amorous adventures."

"And you are confident that what you told Miss Newman is what transpired on the S. S. Netherlands on its last voyage and was the cause of death of the three persons this case is about."

"That is based on my best recollection."

"Mr. LaFontaine, are you aware that the Captain and Mrs. Levin, who was also on the ship, told stories about how the three passengers died that was quite different from your story?"

"Have they?" queried the Purser.

"Yes they have," answered Albert.

"That is surprising," said the Purser, and he glanced in the direction of the Captain who was looking away from him.

Albert was dumbfounded that the presenters of the three conflicting explanations of the travelers' deaths held to their stories. Only one story could be true, and maybe the truth lay somewhere else.

Before proceeding with questions of the ship's crew, Albert chose to bring the Captain to the stand again.

As they crossed paths between the witness box and their seats in the audience, the Captain and Purser looked hard at each other.

Albert resumed his questioning. "Captain Meergossen, three of you tell different stories of the deaths of the deceased passengers on your ship. Do you still insist that your version is the true one?"

The Captain shifted nervously in his seat, drank from a glass of water that had been placed at the witness stand, shook his head, and began to speak. He started off slowly.

"I never thought it would come to all this. I have been a Ship Master for twelve years now, and my record is spotless. I have transported thousands of people across the ocean and through European waterways. I have seen myself not only as a transporter but also as someone who helps to assist people in improving their lives."

He looked toward the ship line officials and nodded, as if looking to them for approval.

He went on: "The job is not an easy one, and many unfortunate things happen aboard a ship. Of course, nothing is worse than people dying. It hurts me when people lose their lives aboard ship and have to be put in the ocean. But there are rules to be followed."

He took out a handkerchief from his back pocket and wiped his brow.

"Yes, when the ladies came to talk to me the other day, I told them their relatives had died of cholera on the ship and were put to sea. Only half of that is true. Yes, they were put to sea. But they didn't die from cholera. Travelers do die from cholera, but not these three."

The audience was buzzing. Judge Smith again asked for quiet.

The Captain turned toward the Judge and continued: "Why did I say that? Well, I knew that the three persons had died from other circumstances, but I could not bring myself to tell the women what really happened. I thought, 'The three travelers are dead. The ladies and their families want to know how it happened, to put their minds at rest. What harm would it do to say they died of cholera? Whatever they died from, they cannot be brought back to life or even their bodies recovered.'

"I guess I made a mistake. In this case, telling the truth would have been terribly difficult for me, and it would have caused pain for the ladies. I meant well. But yes, I did not tell the whole truth."

The crowd in the courtroom was stirring and whispering to each other. The Judge pounded his gavel several times and called for order. He thanked the Captain for his candid statement. "The truth, as difficult as it might have been to tell, would have simplified this case and brought it to resolution a lot sooner."

Albert was a bit taken aback by the Captain's testimony and looked at Sarah with raised eyebrows. He asked permission to approach the bench and was granted it.

"Your Honor," he said in a whisper, "the Captain's statement was a surprise and changes the picture somewhat, but we still don't know what happened on the ship and I would like to continue to question the Captain and other witnesses." The judge concurred.

Before Albert could continue questioning the Captain, Purser LaFontaine stood up and waved his hand toward Albert and the Judge. Getting no immediate response, he called out loudly, "I would like to make a statement, too."

Judge Smith rapped his gavel once more and asked him to be seated. "I will have no more outbursts. This is a court of law and court procedures must be followed."

Albert conferred again with the Judge, after which Judge Smith excused the Captain from the witness stand and asked that the purser be sworn in. Albert then asked the purser if he wished to make a statement.

Purser LaFontaine apologized for his poor English. "Since we hadn't expected to be confronted by the lady or anyone else about how the passengers died, the Captain and I had not discussed how to tell about the deaths. When Miss Newman came to where I was staying and asked about the deaths, I was not prepared to respond. I too made up a story that might have been true.

"I remembered her brother from the ship because he told us he was a pharmacist. I thought that might come in handy if the nurse needed some help with passengers who were sick. I saw on the ship deck that her brother was friendly with Miss Borchowitz and Mister Solomon. It raced through my mind that Newman could have had poison that led to the deaths of the others.

"My imagination even created the situation where there was jealousy among them that provoked Newman. Once all three had died, I decided to tell a story about him trying to poison Solomon, and Miss Borchowitz accidentally becoming a victim. Newman then took the poison himself."

The senior of the two ship line officials stood up and called out "It is not the policy of" before the Judge cut him off and threatened to have anyone who speaks out without being questioned removed from the courtroom. The Judge asked the purser to continue.

"None of that was true. It was only in my imagination. In fact, the killings were brutal but didn't involve poison. Like the Captain, I just wanted to give an explanation of the deaths that would close the discussion. I am sorry I caused problems. I meant well. Maybe I should have been a mystery writer instead of a purser." Several in the courtroom laughed nervously.

The purser wanted to continue speaking but Albert told the Judge to have the purser step down. Sarah was stunned but relieved that Julius was no longer a murder suspect. Albert appeared perplexed but satisfied that his investigation supported the new statements of both the Captain and the purser.

He needed to move the hearing to a conclusion, so Albert asked for the Captain to return to the stand. Judge Smith agreed but told Albert to proceed with haste.

"Captain Meergossen, you have already corrected your statement about your conversation with Sarah Newman and Sheyna Goetz. Now tell me what you know about the deaths of the three people on your ship."

"Ach, this is the most difficult part," said the Captain. "When I was called to the steerage area because a woman's scream was heard by some of the passengers, followed by screams of men, the purser who had already gotten there described what he found. The nurse examined the three bodies and confirmed the deaths. I looked at the scene. It was awful. My first instinct was to remove the bodies and clean up the mess. We needed to restore order to the ship and make it seem to the other steerage passengers that the three persons were taken away because they were ill.

"It was possible that one or more passengers did the killing. That would not be unheard of. It's happened on a couple of my trips. We didn't want to talk with the passengers at that time. So we went ahead and talked to the crew. None of them admitted to stealing from, or attacking, the persons.

"One of the crew members spoke up and described what happened. He pointed to one of the others and said he was looking through bags in the steerage area. He said the woman came in when he was opening her bag. When the woman saw that her candelabra was being stolen, she screamed. Two other crew members pushed her away. They claimed she fell and hit her head on a metal post. They said it was an accident.

"Her two men friends came rushing in from the deck area. Three of the crew fought with them and the result was the two men were killed. The crew claimed they were only defending themselves. At least, that's what they told me."

Laments of "Oy, oy" and "Got en Himel" came from a couple of the people in the audience.

"Did one of the crew take the candelabra?" asked the Judge.

"They claimed they didn't. They said as soon as they saw the persons were probably dead they rushed back to their quarters.

"It sickens me to tell all this. I had hoped that when we got back to Holland, I would report what took place and the crew members would face a hearing there. Now it has to come out here."

Albert asked: "Are the crewmen you referred to in the room?" Heads turned in the courtroom. The six men sitting behind the ship line officials began fidgeting. One of them rose and said "I need to go to the toilet." When a police officer moved toward him and motioned for him to sit, he sat down.

The Captain lifted himself partly out of his chair and pointed to three of the men. One was a short fellow with long hair knotted at the back of his head and a dark unshaven face. A second was much taller with light hair. The third was a huge man with a protruding belly covered partly by a knee length canvas coat. He was the one who had previously tried to leave the courtroom.

"Please stand," the Judge ordered the three men. "Bailiff, put these men in custody until further orders."

Judge Smith told how this was an unusual hearing for the court and he would consider that the three men be held on suspicion of murder in a jury trial. He ordered a recess in the hearing until he could talk with Judge Brown and consider a trial date. The crowd moaned. The Bailiff announced a recess.

During the recess, Sarah and Sheyna embraced each other and tears flowed. They had heard a startling amount of new information and they believed the case had been solved.

Then Sheyna asked, "But what happened to the menorah?"

"One of the crew must have it," replied Sarah.

She then turned to Albert. "What would Judge Smith be discussing with Judge Brown?"

Albert told her it must have to do with the ship's personnel not being American citizens.

"What will that have to do with this case?"

"There are not only laws for the United States and for each State and local area; there is also international law. The United States and most other countries respect international law. A decision has to be made as to which law should take precedent if a trial is to be held."

"You mean we may not know the final outcome today or even soon?"

"Let's just wait till the Judge comes back in."

During the recess, Judge Smith had a brief conference with Judge Brown. He then returned to the hearing room and reconvened the court. The three crewmen were brought into the room and seated near the front under close guard.

At that moment, the courtroom door opened and a federal marshal entered, accompanied by a woman. He signaled to the Judge and went to the bench to explain who the woman was.

Judge Smith had her sworn in and seated in the witness box.

He asked her to identify herself and tell what work she did.

"My name is Bridgit Jorgenson. I am a nurse and came a few days ago on the ship Netherlands."

"Were you on the ship when three persons were reported dead?" asked the Judge.

"Yes, I was."

"Do you know what caused their deaths?"

"The woman appeared to die from a head injury. The two men had severe bruises and numerous knife wounds on their bodies and had bled to death."

"Do you know how those fatal injuries happened—who was responsible?"

"No, I don't know."

"Do you know the three crew members in the front of this room?"

"Of course. We worked together on the ship."

"Did you speak with them after the three bodies were put to sea?"

"Yes, several times."

"Did any of them talk about what happened to the three persons?"

"They didn't tell me about that. But the one in the coat over there—he told me to take something off the ship after it docked."

The federal marshal came forward with a large pouch and whispered to Judge Smith.

"Miss Jorgenson, is that your pouch?"

"Yes, it is."

"And what is in it?"

"A silver candelabra."

The audience stirred.

"Is the candelabra yours?"

"No. It was given to me by that fellow in the coat. He said to hide it somewhere until he could come for it."

"And you did?"

"Yes, and I hid myself too. I realized where it came from. I didn't want to be involved with something stolen, but I was afraid of him. I should have come forward sooner."

Judge Smith thanked her and asked her to step down and be seated at a table.

"This has been upsetting. It is obvious that crimes have been committed. However, the criminal acts took place on the high seas. According to international law, this case cannot be brought to trial in this jurisdiction. It has to be referred to an international tribunal, probably somewhere in Europe, or to a court in the Netherlands."

He ordered the crew members released to the ship, with the understanding that they and the rest of the ship's personnel would leave the country as soon as possible. They would be monitored by federal marshals until they left.

"I will inform the U.S. immigration authorities what has transpired and order that these ship personnel not be permitted to enter the country again," he informed those present.

Albert spoke up. "Your Honor, it would be fitting to give the candelabra to Mrs. Goetz, who was a relative of Rivka Borchowitz. She can see that it is returned to her family."

"That would be appropriate," said the Judge.

It was nearly five o'clock. Light from outside the courtroom was fading. With the doors open, noises of marine traffic could be heard from the East River.

Just as the Judge was concluding his statement, Molly appeared at the door. Her curiosity had been torturing her. When she got off work, she raced to the courthouse to find out what had happened there. When she learned what had taken place, she embraced Sarah and exchanged fond words with the families and friends of the deceased in the room.

There were great sighs of relief from the Newman and Goetz families, even though their hearts were heavy with the loss of their loved ones. Sarah went to Albert and, shaking his hand, thanked him for all his efforts.

Albert made clear to all who listened that the case would ultimately have to be resolved in Europe but that the new evidence pointed to the guilty parties. "As for the families here," he said, "the case can be considered closed. What happened to Julius, Abe, and Rivka has been determined."

The stress of the case had been building up for Albert. Until now, he had remained detached from the goings on, as a lawyer should, and stayed relatively calm about his investigation and the hearing. All of a sudden, it all came crashing down on him.

Sarah noticed his discomfort when he elected to step away and sit down on a nearby chair. "Do you feel sick?" she asked. When he assured her he was going to be all right, she smiled and threw her arms around his neck. Embarrassed for a moment, he rose from the chair and returned the hug.

When he collected himself, Albert told Sarah that, when the time for grieving was over, he would like to see her again. She nodded her head. "Sure," she remarked, "that would be nice."

Mr. Newman took Albert aside and shook his hand. "Lots of thanks. I guess I owe you some money."

"I'm very sorry about Julius. It must be awful losing your only son."

"Yes, but he now rests in peace. I hope the murderers will be punished."

"I hope so, too," Albert replied, handing Nathan his calling card. "As for my charges, let's see, there's the cost of transportation, paper and pencils, and a couple of lunches. That comes to about four dollars and fifty cents. You can pay me later."

"But what about your time?"

"Oh yes, my time. What I'd like to do is forget the charges for my time if you invite me to dinner at your house when Sarah is there."

"Aha," Nathan said, "I can see why you're a good lawyer," and they blended in with the rest of the crowd.

978-0-595-39650-4
0-595-39650-X

Printed in the United States
70879LV00003B/326